THE FIRST EARTH WARRIOR

BY
MICHELE CALLENDER

Publisher's Cataloging-in-Publication Data

Names: Callender, Michele, author.
Title: The first earth warrior / by Michele Callender.
Description: New York, NY: Michele Callender, 2020.
Identifiers: LCCN: 2020915828 | ISBN: 978-1-7355913-2-2
(Hardcover) | 978-1-7355913-1-5 (pbk.) | 978-1-7355913-0-
8 (ebook)
Subjects: LCSH Good and evil--Fiction. | Warriors--Fiction.
| Fantasy. | Christian fiction. | BISAC FICTION /
Christian / Fantasy
Classification: LCC PS3603.A44624228 F57 2020 | DDC
813.6--dc23

Ebook ISBN: 978-1-7355913-0-8

Paperback ISBN: 978-1-7355913-1-5

Hardcover ISBN: 978-1-7355913-2-2

Library of Congress Control Number: 2020915828

MicheleWrites2@Gmail.com

Dedication

I THANK GOD FOR MAKING MY LIFE AN
ADVENTURE WORTH LIVING.

Contents

The Nameless One

When he was born, he was considered one of the Earth-Stained Ones to the people in the plains. He was a descendant of the dark hairless people who were thought to be extinct. Others thought that they existed only in myths. The Plains People were amazed that the child governed the earth at will. He communicated with it, and even became one with it. All that he did could not be explained, therefore he went unnamed.

He was cherished and revered. The Plains People treated him like a king. With his wisdom and guardianship, he succeeded all the chiefdoms before him. Though he never acknowledged a title and was never given a name, he remained great among them through many generations without aging as the others had. Eventually, those among him began to live longer from the blessing that was on him.

When he was not quite a man, his mother died as a very old woman and an elder of the tribe among the Plains People, making him the last of his kind. That day was the first time in his life he felt loneliness.

*****

Many years later, on a cool morning while his beasts were grazing, he was approached by a band of men. When the King of The Hills People sought to make war with the Plains People, the Nameless One faced one of his greatest tests.

"I hear that you are the king!" exclaimed the King of the Hills People as he rode toward the Nameless One on his warring beast. His beast bellowed, exposing sharp metal teeth, rattling the chains across its chest and legs as the king gripped leather harnesses tightly around its neck.

"I've heard that it has been a long time since you've replaced the last *real* leaders of these people. My people have lived in the hills for centuries and all I've ever heard about these people are their herds of grazing beast and the stranger who leads them. I'm disappointed in the myths of these Plains

People. I expected to defeat a powerful, very old man, but I see only a mere bald boy."

The Nameless One looked at the towering beast that was bound by thick hide straps and metal and knew that this man had been taught how to use the substances of the earth from dark places that were far beyond the hills. Transforming ores into instruments of war were the customs of those who lived among fire. The Nameless One knew what drove this man was more than what could be seen.

"Where have you heard of me, and why do you call me a king?" the Nameless one asked.

"It certainly isn't because there is anything magnificent about you!" replied the king with disdain. "You merely resemble a hairless mule with the color of the earth beneath my feet. Yet they follow *you* and deny **me**!" He tossed the head of a Plains People tribesmen at the Nameless One's feet.

"His eyes revealed your whereabouts in death when his tongue refused in life," he mocked. The Nameless One fell to his knees over the head of his friend. The King of the Hills People laughed.

"Raider Clan, do you see this?" he shouted victoriously towards them. He turned toward the Nameless One. "I must admit that you are a good king. You know your place and have now bowed to me! Teach your tribesmen to do the same, and they will not have to suffer like this obstinate fool has."

As the Nameless One picked up his tribesmen's head, a cool breeze arose as though from nowhere. The grass was still, but the unraveled ends of his friends head covering began to wave. The Nameless One's beasts had ceased their grazing and began to howl. The tears that had wet his face had dried, and as the king and his Raiders watched, his friend slowly disappeared in his hands right before their eyes and was carried off by the breeze.

The Raiders' beasts reared up in the air onto their multiple hind legs and spun in panic. They fought to retreat against their rider's violent protests of whipping and tugging of their reins. The Nameless One's beasts continued to howl fiercely.

"What kind of sorcery is this?" cried out the king.

The Nameless One stood. "For the sake of my friend I'll ask you to leave these plains in peace and never return," he said calmly.

4

The king laughed in response. "I see that you are no wiser than him!" he exclaimed as he reached for his sword. "I'll have to claim your head along with his!"

Immediately, the howls of the grazing beasts ceased. The king charged toward the Nameless One and swung his sword. The Nameless One ducked under his arm, avoiding the blow, and struck the beast with his shoulder. The blow was so hard that the warring beast flew onto its side, pinning the king under it and crushing him. Startled as they watched this one man move such a massive animal, the Raiders rushed to defend their fallen leader. The Nameless One reached down and picked up blades of grass in his hand, and, as he did, they hardened into needle-sharp steal. As the Raiders rode closer, one by one the blades of grass under their feet became as sharp as the blades in The Nameless One's hands. They pierced the hooves of the beast that carried them. The men who fell with them were impaled.

Shrieks of pain echoed across the plains. The Raiders that were in the rear were forced to halt their attack as more sharp blades sprang up to form a high barrier around them. A few retreated screaming "Sorcery!" The ground swallowed them up so quickly that all that could be heard were the screams of men in horror.

The sun glinted off the long blades of sharp grass that the Nameless One had in his hands as he walked towards the King of the Hills People. The king struggled beneath his dead beast. His eyes widened as he heard the Nameless One approach.

"Don't come any closer, demon!" he spat in agony with his face pressed against the ground. "I will be avenged. I have ten sons who will come, and they will wear the skin of you… and your descendants… on the bottom of their…sandals," he growled out between gasps.

The Nameless One laughed. "I pray that they are wiser than their father," he said as he squatted down beside him. The king snarled in response to his words.

"Raiders!" the Nameless One called as he stood to face those that were still alive. "Bring his sons to me, but do not be deceived. I'm not limited to this land. Return quickly! Tell them that their father is dying."

As the king struggled to free himself, the sharp blades of high grass softened again into lush green blades that swayed gently in the wind. The Raiders did as he commanded with haste and terror. Their beasts ran so fast that mounds of dust lifted and were all that could be seen in the distance. The Nameless One returned to the dying king.

"I will let your sons visit here where you will be buried. I don't want to destroy them for your deeds. If they seek true peace, they will have it," he said as he gently stroked the blades that he had made sharp between his fingers. "I will tell them that my anger ends with you if they choose well, but if not, then nothing that comes from you or even resembles you in mind, body or spirit will be able to stand against me, let alone my descendants."

"I will see you in the fiery catacombs beneath!" the king yelped in pain. "Why don't you kill me now?" he spat out in fierce anger as he gasped for air. The Nameless One ignored him and tended to his beasts who were still in the fields grazing.

The Reluctant King

By midafternoon, the Raiders returned with nine children on their beasts and a woman who carried a baby on her back. The Raiders removed them from their beasts and lined them up before the Nameless One. The children clung to one another, crying, with fear in their eyes. The oldest son wasn't quite a man yet, but his eyes showed understanding as he looked upon his father with shock and then anger. He glared at his father, who clung to consciousness under the beast with his face to the earth. The woman carrying the baby, the youngest of his wives, wept as she held the child close.

"Remove your sandals. The Nameless One commanded as he looked them over. They did as they were instructed, and for those who were too small to do it for themselves, were violently prompted by the Raiders who had brought them. The Raiders moved away as The Nameless One stood in front of them examining each child in turn.

The children shivered. "Is this king your father?" the Nameless One asked the children old enough to understand as the younger ones began to cry and clung to the older ones.

"He is my father, but he is no king!" said the oldest angrily with tears in his eyes. "Why would a king kill farmers, women and children?"

"Why indeed?" responded the Nameless One. "He said that you and your brothers would avenge him, so I thought I'd give you an opportunity."

"We're still too young!" the oldest one replied, stunned, as the others gasped. "I don't want to fight, especially for him!" he cried as his father's eyes opened slightly at the sound of his scream.

"I don't want to die!" cried out another son.

"Neither do I!" wailed another.

"Why can't we go home?" cried another as the Raiders quieted them with a hiss, a signal that they were accustomed to causing the children to become instantly afraid. *These people rule with fear*, the Nameless One thought.

The woman fell on her knees, pleading with him. "I beg you to spare my son. He is just a baby and knows nothing about war. I will do anything that you ask, but please do not punish children for the sins of their father." The Nameless One perceived they were sincere and nodded.

"Your father will be buried here. I told him that as long as you seek peace you will have it," he told the children. "But…there is another matter." He turned toward the Raiders. "Your king has murdered a man who had three small sons of his own and now there's no one to provide for them in the fields."

"I will do it!" Cried the eldest son abruptly, who wasn't quite a man yet.

"If you are too young to fight, how will you provide for a household?"

"I will learn to plant a thousand fields with my bare hands before I pick up a sword in my father's honor!" he replied.

"Then you will stay and do what you have said on behalf of the woman and children who have suffered today until the children have grown."

The boy's younger siblings cried and protested but the eldest son was unmoved. He glanced at his father's limp body lying under the dead beast and scowled. The Nameless One perceived that the children had none of their father's pride.

"Are there any among you who would like to honor your father today by killing me since your father is now dead?" They all gasped as they glanced at their father again and shook their heads. He smiled, called out to the Raiders, and commanded them. "Take these children back to their mothers and take responsibility for them as if they were your own sons. Raise them to be men who defend their land, nurture it, and not to take from others. This boy will remain here for the burial of his father and to fulfill his vow. What is your reply to my request?"

"Yes, Good King!" They replied in unison and bowed their heads. The woman who had begged him for mercy bowed toward him in gratitude while weeping. She wrapped her child onto her back with a cloth and mounted the beast that she had shared with one of the Raiders. The other Raiders gently gathered all the other children and rode off toward the hills with less urgency. The boy watched as his brothers rode away. He waved and smiled to calm those who were wailing as he yelled out in his native tongue, "Trait min! I'm away!" The Nameless One waited as he waved until they were out of sight.

"It is time to bury him," the Nameless One said when the boy turned to face him again. The boy walked to his father's body and tried to push the beast off him with his hands. When he realized that it was impossible, he lay on his back and tried to kick it off with his feet. The Nameless One watched with amusement at the boys' determination. When he saw that his efforts were in vain, he tried to pull his father out from under the beast by his hand and saw that he wouldn't budge. He then began to dig under his father with his hands, frantically scraping the earth with his nails pulling up grass and rocks until his fingers were sore. As the sun slowly set, he found rocks and sticks and tried to use them as tools to break the earth. Eventually, exhausted and frustrated, he fell back onto his back, breathing heavily. Wiping the sweat from his brow he realized that the small ditch he created around his father and the towering beast that blanketed him could hardly be considered a grave. Finally, the Nameless One asked, "What do they call you boy?"

"Illiam, Good King," he said as he rose to his knees to kneel in front of him.

"Why do you call me Good King?"

"I call you king because you defeated my father and his men. No one has been able to stand against him. Also, I call you a Good King because that is what the Raiders said that my father called you with his own mouth before he died. I heard them say that he mocked you after killing your tribesman and called you good. My father was no king because he killed the innocent. I feel safe here with you. If you were him my head would be stuffed and swinging from your belt by now."

Illiam shrugged. "He had taken the land from many villages and increased his territory," he continued tonelessly. "My mother lived along the Great River but, he killed my grandfather and her tribesman in order to make her his wife. He told her that I'm to be the first of many sons."

"Get up boy and follow me," the Nameless One said, agitated from listening to the boy's recollection of his father's atrocities as he began to walk toward his village. His beasts followed him.

"But, what about my father?" the boy asked in confusion. "You told me that I must bury him."

"We'll let the dead bury itself," he replied.

"But I must fulfill my oath!" the boy cried out, proving to the Nameless One that even at a young age, he was more honorable than his father. Without turning around, the Nameless One released the sharp blades of grass from his hands, causing the earth to swallow the boy's father and the beast that trapped him before they reached the ground. The boy saw and was astonished. He quickly ran to the spot where his father was buried and laid a few small stones on the ground to mark it. He ran to catch up to the Nameless One without looking back.

This is my friends' replacement Great One? The eldest boy of a cruel and greedy man? The Good King asked in a silent prayer. *Who is this Good King? If it is me…please help me to watch over him well!* The Nameless One strode ahead, followed by Illiam, who struggled to match his pace.

When the Good King returned to his village, he introduced Illiam to the elders and his fellow tribesman. Illiam was instantly hated and feared by most. "Why is he here?" Yelled out many tribesmen. "Others will come because of him!" Called out another. Some even picked up rocks to kill him, but one glance from the Nameless One discouraged them.

Seeing their distress, Illiam fell on his knees. "I am here to pay my father's debt," he said boldly. "I vow to fulfill my years caring for the family who lost their provider today for as long as the Good King has requested."

"Good King?" Asked a powerful voice from one elder as he and the other council members emerged from the crowd to stand before them. He then turned to look among his fellow council members and declared, "What a befitting name!" They all nodded in unison. It was established at that moment that not only was Illiam's obligation accepted, but with his arrival, they were able to give a name to their blessed, kind, and unusual leader.

A Vow Fulfilled

Several years had passed. Illiam grew stronger and wiser each year. He was faithful and just as eager to fulfill his oath as the day he took it. He learned everything that was taught to him quickly from neighboring farmers who were willing to accept him, but many were wary, believing that it was impossible for a man's nature to be far from his father's. Despite his struggles, the children of the household grew tall and were well able to follow in their father's footsteps and claim the inheritance of the land and wealth cultivated by the son of their enemy. The eldest was just a year younger than Illiam but learned well and even befriended him. If it weren't for the company of the Good King many wouldn't have acknowledged him at all. The king began to invite Illiam to attend meetings among the elders and granted him a seat beside him as village issues were raised and resolved. Illiam began to follow the Good King everywhere and listened to the stories passed down to him by the king's mother about the origin of their people. He learned how the Good King was the first of their people to be born among the People of the Plains and how the Great One provided for them and all that were his.

"I was born of a tribe of nomads," said the Good King. "My people survived by living off the kill of large beasts that populated the unbearably hot marshes and jungles around them. Their numbers grew around the surrounding areas to the west of the Great River but were hunted by what they didn't understand. My mother fled when she was still carrying me in her womb. She was separated from our people by an ambush while she attempted to gather the remnant of a beast from a fresh kill. To her surprise, she found herself running frantically through the thickness of the trees from a frightening foe she could hear but couldn't see. The predator chased her for what seemed like hours. It shook the ground, rattled trees, and startled the flying beasts that instantly flew into the air. Finally, she found her way out from among the trees and thick vines to find that the invisible creature was no longer pursuing her.

All was silent as she peered into the dense darkness of thick trees that separated her from everything and everyone that she knew. She attempted to go back into the jungle after a day or so to rejoin our family, but the noise commenced as soon as she attempted to venture in too deeply. Her next attempt was hindered when the jungle closed even more becoming a wall of thick branches, leaves and thorns almost pushing her toward the green plush plains before her. In the heat of that day she collapsed from hunger and exhaustion, realizing that she was now left alone with a child in her womb. In order for us to survive, she had to move forward."

The Good King seemed as young as Illiam was who was then 18, but his wisdom surpassed them all.

*****

Over time, Illiam yearned to learn more about the Great One that had communicated and protected the Plains People. He would follow the Good King and would silently watch him as he prayed. The king would sit or sometimes lay on his face for hours. Illiam saw how The Good King reigned over them without force or even a desire to be acknowledged as anything more than a fellow tribesman. He behaved more like a guardian, a protector who quietly cared for the life of everyone around him. Illiam admired him. He was especially fascinated by the Good King's ability to control the earth. He even saw him merge into the environment around him when a flood threatened to destroy the village just before harvest season.

On that day, the Good King stood at the base of the stream during a heavy rain. As the winds raged, the waters rushed past him as he stood. The waters rushed in and began crashing against the riverbanks, swelling up causing villagers to leave their homes nearby as they attempted to collect and move their beasts as far away from the floodwaters as possible. Some sought to move them to higher ground along the plains, but mudslides began collapsing homes and dragging them into the uncontrollable floodwaters. The Good King remained still as the waters rose to his waist. He closed his eyes in a prayer as he lifted his head towards the sky, raised his hands in front of his chest as if he were enjoying the rain that was pounding down on him. He spread his arms out and brought his hands together with a tremendous clap that resounded like thunder. Lightning flashed and the earth underneath him groaned and shifted. The ground shook as it rose into a high cliff against the rapidly rising floodwaters, raising everything that sat on it.

Illiam ran to the edge of the rising bank and peered over the edge to see what had happened to the Good King who was standing in the midst of the flood below. He was amazed to see that the floodwaters had overtaken him and carried him down the raging stream. Illiam ran along the cliff, calling out to him in fear. The rain began to cease, but the floodwaters continued to carry the Good King down toward the valley where the river that was once a stream ended and a waterfall's drop began. He cried out again and ran faster, trying to race the waters. When he looked again, he no longer saw him. Illiam stopped and panted as he eagerly scanned the waters, and still the king was gone.

"No!" Illiam cried out in despair. He ran with all the strength he had left, slipping on the wet earth while trying not to fall off the cliff into the waters himself. He reached the edge of the cliff where the waterfall dropped. He peered as far down the falls as he could. He looked to see if anything in the mist and foam resembled the body of the one he so respected, but he saw nothing. He dropped to his knees in despair.

"Great One…" he wept. "Why didn't you save your blessed one?" The waters made a tremendously unusual sound below that caused him to crawl to the edge of the cliff to see what was happening. As the muddy floodwaters quieted and continued to wash over the waterfall, a warm, calming breeze grazed his cheeks drying them from the tears that were streaming down his face. Suddenly a strong wind blew towards the sky, causing a dense mist to rise into the air from the waterfall itself. The waterfall began to flow in the opposite direction. The force was so great that it pushed Illiam onto his back in the mud, completely wetting his face again and blurring his vision. He wiped his eyes with his hands and saw the mist form in front of him into a man.

"What made you run so desperately boy?" the Good King asked.

"Good King…you saw me?" he asked astonished. "But… I saw you taken away!"

"I was guiding the floodwaters away and have just returned," the Good King replied, amused.

"You have unimaginable power!"

"The Great One is the source of All power."

"How can I have these abilities? Will he give some to me?"

"Why do you want them?" the king asked, as he left the cliff and began walking back towards the village. "Remember boy, there is no room here for sorcery."

Illiam stood in shock, not at the Good King's reply but how anxious he was when he saw what he could do. He then followed him with even more zeal as he carefully considered the question that was posed to him, "Why do I want them?"

*****

Illiam was now a young man who had begun to gain notoriety from the village elders - as well as their daughters- as a trustworthy and noble man.

"Although he is like a stranger to me, I have to admit that the boy has provided well for our neighbor's household," one elder said.

"Better than most of us, honestly speaking," replied another.

"Remember, he is still the eldest son of a murderer. It's because of the Great One's mercy that we are able to live in peace with his kind among us," interjected another.

"How long would it take for the boy to prove himself? How long will you continue to call that young *man* a boy?" asked another elder to the first.

"I am old, every man is a boy to me," he replied.

"Then what are you to me?" asked the Good King as he entered the meeting.

"You are the wisest among us all, Good King. Therefore, I ask what should we do with him now that he has fulfilled his sworn duty? Do we let him live here or do we cast him out? I vote for the latter respectfully," proposed the first elder.

"And I say that he has earned his right to stay if he chooses," proclaimed another. "He has embraced our ways and he is at peace here."

"Will he marry here? Maybe one of your granddaughters or daughters!" one shrewd elder proclaimed mockingly.

"Yes, I've overheard a few of the young women talking. Many are quite impressed with his looks and his demeanor. He is a determined young man, and I dare say, kind. What he has done for our neighbor and his household is very impressive and shouldn't be overlooked," insisted another.

"I agree," stated one elder who rarely spoke, but stood up from his seat to announce, "I would be honored to have him as my neighbor. He respects the earth and prosperity follows him." In shock the room grew still, then elders began to murmur among themselves until another voice among them said, "I second it! Although his father was an animal," he acknowledged. "He has shown that he is not his son in spirit."

"My dear members, I appeal to you that you take into consideration all the possibilities. You never know how his father was when he was his age. He could have been handsome, dependable, and well-mannered as this boy or man, as you say, is. But…It is possible that his true nature we have not yet seen. Let him return to his people. If he returns and continues to find peace among our people, then he can dwell with us if it pleases him. If not, let him stay where he belongs, among his own kind," recommended the first elder earnestly.

"How long will you be indifferent to strangers?" asked the Good King addressing council. The room grew silent.

"Until we no longer lose our heads for our lands, Good King," said the youngest among them. "I'm still afraid and so are our families!"

"You speak the truth. You are afraid…but have you considered that a plan and a purpose is being fulfilled before your eyes? No threat like that has visited our land before or since," stated another.

"But now that it has, how can we ever trust a stranger again?" he asked.

"How could you ever trust me? Have you forgotten that my mother was a stranger to your ancestors?" the Good King asked. "He will return to his people, but he is free to return to us if he chooses."

*****

Illiam was sitting outside the meeting place as he watched each of the elders file out one by one. He stood up quickly from where he was sitting and bowed to all as they exited. Some avoided his eyes completely. Some grabbed his hand or smiled but very few returned the gesture. There were 21 altogether in that generation. The Good King was the last to greet him.

"Come and follow me, boy," the Good King beckoned.

"You are released from your vow and may return to your people among the hills."

"Good King, if nothing has changed, I may be asked to reign in my father's place."

"Then consider ruling them well," the Good King replied.

"But I am a stranger to them. I've grown to love this *land*, *your* people and *your* God. Their trades are different from what I've learned here. Also, their customs and beliefs were barbaric and cruel. How can I not make many enemies?" Illiam asked anxiously.

"You may, but you may also make a few friends. Your few can be greater than their many. Consider your family you have left behind. For their sakes visit them," the Good King responded calmly.

"Yes, Good King I will go back to them but, I hope to return again. The plains have become my home. Although I miss my brothers and my mother I want to stay here among the people of the plains. How can I deny such a blessed place? A peaceful place. I could never be thankful enough for it."

"There is one last thing, Illiam, that I must do before we part," the Good King said as he placed his hand on his shoulder. Illiam froze in shock. Not from his touch but for the fact that the Good King had called him by name for the first time, or so he thought. When he awoke, he was in his bed and the sun of the new day was shining down on him in his little resting place that he had built in the field that he had nurtured for years.

The Unknown Journey Home

Illiam started down the path that morning that he had traveled many years before when he and his brothers were first brought to the plains. The road became narrower as he walked farther away from the land that he'd nurtured and loved towards the place that brought back the memories that he hated. The road had been covered with brush, trees and grass that had grown so high that he had to extend his arms out to push it out of his way to find a clearing to the path toward the hills. As he continued, he saw that there were very large trees that weren't there before that were along the boundaries of the plains as he peered up at the large hills before him. The tall grass had finally disappeared under his feet to dry cracked earth that sloped upwards towards his destination. Disappointment grew inside of him. His father had left him with a legacy of shame for a debt that he felt was still not fully paid for, no matter how much he sacrificed. His heart grew heavy with every step. He wanted to be obedient to the Good King but knew in his heart that he would never be satisfied with the life that his people of his past had led. *Great One, I'll go, but please make it possible for me to return to you and your people. I'm yours now.*

He encouraged himself by imagining what he would do when he returned. He thought about his mother and brothers visiting him and learning the ways of a peaceful nation. He never considered a wife for himself, but he considered helping other households in need, and imagined how he would help provide for them. His thoughts trailed as he hiked up the steep hills that plateaued often, then inclined again as he looked back once more. He tried to remember the last thing that the Good King said. "There is one last thing Illiam…" He couldn't remember the rest. "What was it? And how embarrassing was it that I fainted?" he recalled to himself. "It had to be the absolute first time he called me by my name, and something other than "boy"… and my consciousness wasn't present to enjoy it!" he complained in humiliation. He stopped and let out a disparaging huff as he shook his head, adjusted his load of provisions that he carried in a sack with him on his back and continued forward.

Illiam returned to his village among the hills by the mid-morning of the following day. Many things had changed as he entered the town. The huge pillars mounted by urns of fire that marked the entrance to the village were gone. The houses that were fortified with heavy timber and metal gates were now opened to beautiful gardens. The sound of children's screams of laughter chimed so loudly that Illiam quickly turned to brace himself as he searched to see where it was coming from. The knot within his stomach loosened slightly when he saw them running behind him as they chased one another with thick colorful strings in their hands, but he remained very alert. He hadn't arrived at his mother's house yet. That fear still hadn't disappeared. A beast belted out a howl when a stray hound nipped at its set of four rear legs. Its owner shewed it away with the edge of his speared walking stick and laughed. "You'll eat tonight hound. Don't you worry. I'll make sure of it. No one and nothing will starve here anymore." As Illiam looked above the man's head, he saw the words "Lems Slouts, Towns Butcher" written over him on a large stretch of sheared hide.

Illiam looked around for someone he knew. There were many unfamiliar faces and the streets were much more crowded than he remembered. He also wondered if anyone would be able to recognize him. It soon became obvious that those who passed by only noticed him when they wanted to sell him something. Women were dressed in long tunics and colorful scarves tied around their shoulders and waists. Their necks were beaded, and many had metal jewelry dangling from their hair and ears. They carried their goods of breads and vegetables strapped to their sides or over their shoulders with larger pieces of colorful fabric. The men were dressed in loose colorful tunics tied with thick cords around their waists. Fabric was wrapped around the woven belts that made pockets of different sizes to hold their money and goods. Two men with dark clothing watched him through the crowds of people. Their tunics were long and were open on the sides up to the hip revealing dark loose pants underneath that covered each leg all the way to their ankles, secured there and tied with string. They were covered all over in this dark material only revealing their eyes, the sandals on their feet, and their metal belts that had sharp knives with symbols etched on them shining in the daylight that were strapped to them. He watched them as they made their way toward him.

"Where are you from stranger?" one of the men asked.

"You men are the strangers. My name is Illiam and I have just returned from the People of the Plains after repaying my father's debt." The men's eyes were broadened as they looked at each other in astonishment. As they looked him over, they saw the resemblance that he had with their older brother Arlan in the north. In amazement they replied, "We did not recognize you. I was just a child when you were taken," said one of the two men.

"Yes, I was just a year older than him when the Good King demanded that we come. We are only two of your younger brothers. Please, come with us!" The other instructed with excitement. With an air of caution Illiam followed them. The youngest of them removed his head covering. "Wait, you shouldn't do that here among the people. Keep on your uniform. We need to maintain order and establish authority," corrected the oldest.

"What does it matter now? The eldest of *all* of us is here!" he replied with delight. He looked at Illiam closely as they walked through the crowds of villagers and merchants as they exited the marketplace. "How is it that we look the same age?" he asked with a familiar accent that Illiam had almost forgotten completely.

"What do they call you?" Illiam asked him to avert the question. He didn't quite know how to answer his inquisitive brother's question because he wasn't too sure himself. Without being offended the youngest of them continued, "I'm Josem from our fathers sixth wife and he's Nabe. The nag."

"The cautious!" Nabe responded, intently correcting his outspoken younger brother again.

"How did you escape the demon?" Josem asked.

"What demon? Are you referring to our father?" Illiam asked.

"Illiam, it's obvious that father wasn't the one who took you. His murderer did."

Illiam stopped and responded abruptly, "If it weren't for father none of us would have had to be taken into that land at all." At that moment, Illiam didn't know if he should be grateful or furious about the events that occurred due to his father's cruelty. His first thought gave him new life and hope, but he had always chosen the latter. "I remember clearly that father pledged his honor, on our infant hearts towards avenging his death against one man who defended his land, and its people by the power of his God. When he offered us

33

an opportunity which one of *you* stepped forward to avenge him?" Illiam asked.

"We were just children!" Josem answered in defense.

"And it seems as though, you still are a child, Josem," Nabe said. "If the Good King was a demon…would we have left with our lives all those years ago? And would Illiam have returned to us?" he asked Josem. "Some things are complicated, and some things are just simple deductions," he calmly said turning to Illiam in agreement.

"You see! A nag," Josem complained, throwing his hands into the air. "How and *why* have you returned to us now, Illiam?"

"I was told to come," Illiam replied.

"Told to come? So, you were really exiled?" Josem asked in shock. Illiam laughed out loudly causing his brothers to stop walking and look at each other curiously.

"Why do you laugh?" Nabe asked.

"It seems *so* doesn't it?" Illiam said with a smile as he thought about the different looks on the council members faces that openly hated him when they exited the meeting that day of the decision. "But, I'm free to return if I please. The Great One is mine and I am his."

"Who is this Great One that I keep hearing about?" Josem asked. "Is that what the People of the Plains call the Good King now? Is he still bald?"

"What difference does his baldness make Josem?" Nabe chided.

"Well, what has he done to you? Were you his slave?" Josem said as he redirected his question.

"Those are ridiculous questions Josem!" Nabe snapped.

Great One... Illiam prayed in amusement as he listened to them bicker on. *I love them already.*

*****

Illiam continued to walk with them as Josem asked every question that came to mind while Nabe listened. Josem eventually stopped his questioning when he saw that Illiam would no longer say a word. They had already led him outside of the marketplace and past small houses made of rocks, clay, and sticks.

"We're here," Josem said as he rushed ahead to a larger house than the others that they had passed. He ran and opened the door while Illiam and Nabe maintained their steady stride toward it. An older woman came out with a plain brown tunic and a colorful scarf draped around her head and neck like what the woman in the marketplace wore. A younger woman followed with two children behind her. Josem came out pushing the crowd forward with his motion of pulling the door shut behind him and quickly nudging his chin up in the direction of Nabe and Illiam. The older woman wrung her hands on a cloth and waited for the two to draw closer. Josem stood before them with a welcoming smile. "This is my mother Ilda and my sisters. The eldest is Fae and the twins are Tulia and Sofni."

Illiam bowed his head as the older woman stepped forward. "I had somehow expected you to be much older than you are right now. You've spent many years away from us...so much has happened since..."

"Is my mother near?" Illiam asked.

"She is far away, but I think that it would be best if I prepare you with a few details of how the culture of our people has changed before you go."

"I look forward to hearing all about it, Isha Ilda, Milady Ilda," he replied humbly.

"Come in, you are welcome," she said as she hurried him inside. Illiam was asked to sit on one of the four chairs that were placed to the rear of the house near the fire pit that was surrounded by blackened fired stones. Ilda took the second seat while Fae and Josem occupied the remaining two. Nabe stood while the children sat on fur rugs on the smooth floor towards the front of the house and started to weave thin reeds together meticulously. Although it wasn't clear what they were making it was apparent that the two young children were experienced and worked very well together. There were long cushions rolled up and tied together. They were propped up in the corner near the large front window on top of a thick wooden bench. Three huge beautifully decorated urns of wine were lined along the wall to the right of the entrance while smaller equally decorated jugs sat beside them with lids on them. The house smelled like roasted meat although there wasn't any food to be seen. The large wooden slab of a table that sat between them was bare except an array of multiple sized candles spread about in the center. It formed beautiful mountains and valleys of colored wax that connected them from their consistent use.

"You must have so many questions," Ilda started. "As Josem has said, I am his mother, but Fae and the twins obviously aren't your father's children. Their father died two years ago from a failed heart. I don't know if you remember, but there are seven of us all together. I was your father's sixth wife and between all of us, we had ten sons. Your mother was the first to bare you and your brother Arlan."

"Yes, I remember that much…and…where are my mother and brother now?"

"Your mother married Mosimer, the Raider who took command after your father was killed. He and the others helped raise all your brothers until they were men as the Good King commanded and then he, Arlan and your mother left our village. All the other Raiders followed him taking their women and children who were willing to go with them. They now live in the Northern Outer Lands which are to the east of the Marshes and just before the Great Mountains. It's a very dangerous place."

"Then who protects you?" he asked.

"We do!" Josem proclaimed proudly. "Both Nabe, I, and our other brothers maintain order here. The Raiders have trained us thoroughly and have left the safety of these hills and its people to us. We're treated like princes."

"Because you ARE!" said Ilda. "Your father was King."

"Once we were old enough, Mosimer said that the Raider's had fulfilled their duty. Arlan went with your mother and he only returns to check on us occasionally. Lately, he has been asking if we've encountered any *strangers*," Nabe added.

"Could we assume that you often receive strangers since your village's market is thriving so well?" Illiam asked.

"Yes, traders and nomads mostly, but the strangers that we are trained to find are not merchants or tradesman," said Nabe.

"Yes, we have spotted Drud scouts recently," Josem said.

"What are Druds?" Illiam asked.

"They're horrible men who mix with beasts who live beyond the Marshes and near the Catacombs of Fire. Their homes are built into the sides of the mountains. I've never seen one, but I've heard that they are somehow the only ones who can stand to live that close to the catacombs. They say the hellish fires and dark air within and surrounding it are unbearable," Ilda answered. "I've been hearing stories of them since I was a child. They're descendants of horrid dark blood thirsty creatures who lived in the mountains in tombs built among the fires deep within they say."

"Those are just tales to scare their enemies, Mother. It's a strategy used to weaken their opponent without having to lift a sword. Let me catch one of them to see if he bleeds like a man or howls like a beast," Josem said sneering. The sound of his words caused his twin sisters to turn and look at him abruptly with shock on their faces. They looked at each other and giggled as a smack landed on his arm from his mother as she gestured for him to lower his voice. "Shh, Josem!" she reprimanded.

"They know how to disguise themselves well," Nabe said in a bit of a whisper. "It's all magic. That's the only way I can describe how we could get so close to them and then they would somehow disappear into the crowd right before our eyes," he continued.

"You believe they use sorcery?" Illiam asked out loud without meaning to. He didn't want to alarm them unnecessarily about the dark beings that worshiped a dark god that he had heard about from the stories that the Good King spoke of. He called them the Wet Ones. He assumed that they were probably more legend than real and was glad when it was quickly dismissed by Josem when he said sarcastically, "No more than what you've probably seen brother on the plains all of these years."

You have no idea, Illiam wanted to reply but realized that his brothers wouldn't have understood what he experienced the way he had. Josem had already demonized the Good King, and Illiam didn't want to debate the matter any further so soon.

"Please stay with us tonight and your brothers will take you early in the morning to journey to the Outer Lands," requested Ilda as she grabbed Illiam's hand warmly. "You must be hungry and tired from your journey. Please stay," she requested as she looked deeply into his eyes.

"Yes, and two more of our brothers are coming to relieve us of our duty before dark. The rest are commissioned to do other tasks. Eventually, you'll get to meet Tosh and Roe." Josem said in hopes to convince him further.

"Your mother and I have been hoping for this day for many years." Ilda said with watery eyes as she gently touched his face.

Illiam nodded with a smile in response as she immediately stood and rushed over to the fire pit to create a fire. She sent Josem out to get more wood and Fae to fetch fresh water as Nabe followed to help her. Ilda knelt on her knees under the large wooden table where they all were sitting and pulled up the floorboards underneath. There she grabbed salted fish from a deep well dug ditch lined with large smooth stones. She had unwrapped the fish that were in two pieces of thick cloth and large leathery leaves and began preparing it. She opened a jar that was filled with grain and began crushing it. "Tulia, Sofni! Sno-le-dem Catzvit, hurry and come. Hand me the oil on the shelf," Ilda requested as she remarkably had already crushed the grains into a fine powder, mixed it with the oil and was kneading it into small cakes all with very skilled hands. She used a very heavy wooden rolling pin that shook the table every time she repositioned it over the cakes thinning each of them out to a rounded shape. The fragrance from the oils she poured on them filled the air and caused Illiam's mouth to water. She had finished preparing them, covered them with a damp cloth that she dipped in water and wrung and placed them on the side by the time Josem returned with the extra wood and added them to the fire. "Fae, fetch the tots from the back of the house Sno-le-dem, Hurry!" Ilda said to Fae as she ran to do as she was told.

Fae had heard of a brave older brother that was taken as a slave in battle from Josem and the others. Although, Josem was too young to remember the details he would interject his thoughts using the little memories he had as he gleaned information from his brothers. She was anxious to see how this stranger would become king as she saw in her quiet dreams. "We only have a few fish left for now. Josem will bring meat when he returns from his duties later." Ilda said as she began to soak and prepare all that she had for Illiam to eat.

*****

Josem and Nabe returned to their posts at the market. Ilda demanded that Illiam lay down after he was full in a niche of a room towards the back of the house. He assumed that it belonged to her because of the delicate lace fabric that hung along the walls and was used to shade the room from the sun as it hung elegantly over the window creating a delicate pattern on the adjacent wall. When he awoke, he saw two very tall men dressed in the same clothing as Josem and Nabe accept one of their tunics were sleeveless revealing his bulging arms. Both men had their heads covered as they stood over him revealing only their eyes. Ilda came in with a slap on the arms for both when she commanded, "Reveal your faces in my house!

Uncover your heads. Sno-le-dem, Now!" The men quickly removed their coverings. Illiam saw that the men were very much the brothers of Josem and Nabe. They both had very dark hair and pointed noses that matched their younger siblings. Their jawlines were defined along their surprisingly fair faces. He couldn't help but to wonder if he made as much of an impression when people looked at him.

Tosh stood a little taller than Roe but with a leaner build. Tosh also had a marking on his right arm in the shape of what looked like the seal of the Raiders. It had the shape of an encircled raven with an array of arrows behind it. Illiam looked up at the two with a bit of amusement. He knew them instantly. He couldn't explain how he had felt a strange knowing and connection with them although he had been separated from them since they were younger.

"You must be Tosh," Illiam said to the taller man towering over him to the left. "And... that would make you Roe," he added, pointing to the man on the right as the men looked at him suspiciously.

"We were told that a stranger was seen here. We came to see who it was before we took our posts. Who is he and how does he know us?" Tosh asked Ilda refusing to address Illiam directly.

"I'll leave you to ask him yourself," she said casually as she walked away. "I have other things to do."

"Who are you stranger?" Tosh asked curtly.

"The fear of strangers is common everywhere I see," Illiam whispered to himself as he stood before them. His brothers adjusted their stance. He observed the temperament of Tosh the most. He noticed that he was the most aggressive of the two.

"I don't ask more than once," Tosh threatened with a hard glare from his pale blue eyes.

"Tosh, don't be so rude. I'm sure Isha Ilda would be wise not to bring someone dangerous into her home," he said to his impatient brother. "What is your name stranger and where are you from?" Roe repeated with less angst.

"I am the eldest son of the former king's first wife Isha Hilda. My name is Illiam…and where I'm from you may remember if you try hard enough." Illiam responded as he waited patiently. Tosh's eyes lit up and grew wide as he slowly started to understand what this young foreigner was telling him.

"You're not…You can't be!" Tosh said in amazement as he looked him over more closely.

"Illiam? How can this be?" Roe cried, just as amazed.

"We thought you were dead!" Tosh yelled as Roe grabbed Illiam into his arms and hugged him weeping. Tosh joined in hugging the two as the men outwardly expressed their surprise and joy. *Great One, If I knew that it would be like this, I wouldn't have been so reluctant to come*, he thought. Illiam and his brothers talked for a short while before they had to leave and relieve their younger siblings from their positions at the gate. They promised that they would hear more about the Good King and the People of the Plains. Illiam would also often mention the Great One but neither of them would acknowledge it.

*****

Illiam ate well as Josem and Nabe returned. His brothers talked and argued about their day at the market. They talked about the taxes that they were required to pay and how many had paid their share persistently late or not at all in comparison. Josem laughed about the flirtatious group of women who often came to get their attention. He also complained about the price of meat from the Towns Butcher and threatened to never buy from him again as Isha Ilda salted, seasoned and packed away the pieces that hadn't been eaten for the next day under her strategically placed floorboards. "You can always hunt for the meat yourselves at any time instead of complaining," she said. Instead they continued to eat what they purchased and drank the wine from the large urns that were standing against the wall until they were full and satisfied.

"We heard that you've met Roe and Tash," Nabe said as he put down his cup. "They'll tell the others about you while Josem and I set out to take you on the journey to see Arlan and your mother in the morning. Things have changed. Everything may not be as you have remembered it, Illiam," Nabe said concerned. Illiam noticed that although Josem called Nabe a nag, he was always displaying a mature sensitivity towards the others around him.

"It's better than I expected it to be so far, brother," he said, smiling to reassure Nabe that he didn't have to worry. Illiam saw in his eyes that he was one of the kindest of his little brothers so far. Nabe then abruptly got up and walked to the door. "Good evening."

"Don't forget to take your share of meat to your mother and brothers," Ilda reminded him as she handed him a small sack of what she had prepared for him to take. She handed the bag to him as he repositioned his head covering over his head and face and left for the night.

"Sleep well, Illiam. We go to the Outer Lands tomorrow," Josem said as they climbed a ladder to reach a niche above the kitchen and his mother Ilda's niche for them to sleep peaceably there. It overlooked the rest of the cottage, including the small identical space of an area above the doorway that his sisters shared opposite them. They were already fast asleep. Josem rolled out the large cushioned bed for them to sleep on. *Great One...* Illiam prayed as he began to lay down beside his brother who was already asleep. *Please protect us on our journey and return me safely back to the People of the Plains.* Immediately afterwards, he drifted off to sleep.

Illiam's Dream

Illiam watched a green dragon swooping in from the north. When it opened its mouth, it bellowed fire and dark smoke. Flapping its four enormous wings, the dragon fanned the smoke over the hill-tops, suffocating the people below it. Illiam stood on the hilltop facing the dragon with his right hand clutching a fistful of the earth. A strong wind suddenly surrounded him and entered his eyes, ears, nose, and mouth. Illiam took a deep breath and blew on the earth in his right hand. It spun violently before him and then attacked the green dragon and the smoke it fanned with its wings.

He awoke abruptly in his dark corner. The room was filled with Josem's quiet snores and the moonlight that flooded the room through the windows above their heads. Josem laughed in his sleep and flexed his feet back and forth. Illiam smiled as he turned over onto his back.

I felt like the Good King a little in that dream, Great One, Illiam thought. He inhaled deeply. *Tomorrow, we journey to see Arlan and my mother. Will they recognize me? Is my mother suffering in the Outer Lands with her Raider husband like she did with my father? What will Arlan's reaction be? Will he be as excited as the others, or will he hate me for abandoning him? Will he understand what I had to do for Father's mistakes?* He stared at the ceiling, becoming more anxious as the hour passed. The moon had changed its position, and he was still wide awake. Maybe I should never have fallen asleep earlier, he thought, folding his arms over his chest. *Never mind, worrying won't change anything anyway.* Exhausted he rolled over again and closed his eyes.

What seemed like minutes later, Illiam woke to the sound of heavy footsteps and a sudden huff behind him. "You Plains People sure can sleep!" Josem complained, fully dressed and kneeling over him. Illiam groaned as he turned toward the brightness of the sun.

"Get up, brother. We have a long way to travel," Josem said as he hopped up effortlessly and headed down the ladder. Illiam sat up, stretching his arms and legs before he stood. He peered over the thick wooden banister, which he assumed was the only thing that kept Josem from falling to the space below as he laughed and ran in his sleep, to see Nabe waving at him from below. Ilda had prepared bread and water for them to eat and provisions of dried roasted meat and water to take on their journey. Before the hour was done the men were off to the Outer Lands.

*****

Illiam followed his brothers farther and farther up the steep hillsides for what seemed like days, although it had only been a few hours. Their pace was steady, and they rarely looked back to see if he was keeping up with them. He was used to this from many years of walking behind the Good King. Illiam knew that on a good day he would be able to out climb, out run, and most certainly out walk his confident younger brothers, but his lack of sleep was getting the best of him. The sun was high, and his head began to throb. He decided to rest and quench his thirst.

"Wait!" he panted. "I need a drink."

"Oh, come on eldest!" We've just started our journey! If we stop too many times, we won't get there until the end of next harvest."

"Is it really that far? Illiam panted as he sat on the flattest part of the ground he could find and opened his skin of water to gulp down a mouthful, swishing it back and forth before finally swallowing. Nabe sat down next to him and reached into his small sack for a small sliver of dried meat. "Not you too, Nabe!" Josem complained.

"Don't worry about Josem too much Illiam. He's anxious to get there for reasons much different than ours," said Nabe with a wink. They shared a smile as they watched Josem pace back and forth as he waited for them to rest.

"Come sit with us, Jos. She won't melt if you leave her too long." Nabe teased with a hearty laugh.

"I refuse to delay another minute longer," Josem complained as he began to ascend the hill without them.

"We should go," Nabe said. "He visits often and knows the way much better than I do." Illiam rose with a nod and followed, suddenly feeling refreshed and amused.

*****

The morning light gradually lit their way as the three brothers resumed their journey to the Outer Lands. When Illiam looked back to see how far he had climbed he was amazed at the vastness of the hills. He was able to see as far as the crest of huge trees that were nurtured by the Great River to the west. *Oh Great One...* he prayed inwardly, *this is a beautiful land. May this land continually reflect your majesty.*

"Come along, Illiam! We can't afford to lose another day!" Josem called as they entered the slough of muddy waters of the wooded Bog. The roots of huge trees protruded under their feet, and they were enveloped by the overwhelming heat and stench of the dense muck that separated the land of the Hills People and the Southern Outer Lands. The Bog smelled of tree sap, mold, and death all at the same time. The three drew closer together, cautiously weaving through the mire and low-hanging vines. Thin rays of light gleamed through the thick canopy. Illiam's heart raced at the loud, unrelenting sounds of strange animals lurking in the shadows. Josem and Nabe silently extracted their sharp three-ridged daggers from the straps under their tunics and placed them inside their sleeves. Josem also placed something sharp in his mouth as he looked around for danger. Illiam pulled out a small dagger that had no uniquely designed ridges but had been extremely useful for slitting the throat of a beast that preyed on the grazing beasts on the land that he cared for on the plains. Although he was no hunter, he felt strangely secure with his brothers near him.

Raiders of the Southern Outer Lands

J ust before nightfall, their clothes caked with mud and dirt, the three brothers stumbled into the first camp built beside The Lake That Provides. The lake was named as a refuge for the sect of the Raider Clan that had decided not to travel any farther north. Josem and Nabe were greeted with hugs and laughter. Nabe turned toward Illiam who stood far behind them and introduced him to the Commander of the Southern Raider Clan.

"Josepher, this is our brother Illiam." The crowd grew silent in mixtures of confusion and shock. "Hilda's child?" an older woman gasped as she covered her mouth in astonishment. She walked over to him and held his face. "Yes, you have your mother's eyes!" She embraced Illiam as he shot his brothers an embarrassed look.

"Come!" she said, grabbing him by the arm and pulling him into the crowd of on-lookers. "It's Isha Hilda's child! He was taken but has been returned. Our king's eldest child has returned!" The crowd touched, embraced, and examined Illiam. The men and women were welcoming and warm.

"How is it possible for you to return and yet be so young?" Josepher asked.

"That's what I asked!" said Josem in jest.

"The Good King...did he curse you? Are you here to deliver his revenge on us?" random voices called from the crowd.

"Our debt is settled," Illiam replied as the guilty knot in his stomach tightened. *"Nothing is settled. How could it be? What is a life of labor in return for someone's life? Your father's line should be cut off, murderer!"* said a voice in his mind, so loudly that he glanced around to see where it was coming from. He was relieved that that no one else could see his torment. He had learned how to conceal it through the many years he had spent working among the Plains People. The louder it became the harder he worked, but Illiam was shocked as the voice grew angrier than ever. Never had he heard the word so clearly...*MURDERER!*

As his father's heir, Illiam felt that the responsibility for the king's wrongs was his to bear. He couldn't rest until he did. His eyes burned, and he swallowed hard. As his cheeks began to warm, he found it too hard to concentrate on any of the questions the Raiders and their families asked out of their pure joy and curiosity.

Josem maneuvered through the crowd to help Illiam circumvent the crowd's overwhelming probing.

"Good enough people, good enough! Allow him to rest. I knew that you would be surprised to see your eldest prince alive and well, but I must admit that I'm becoming a little...jealous!" he said drawing the crowd's attention as Nabe and Josepher grabbed Illiam by both arms and escorted him toward the large tall tent before them. "Wasn't it just a month ago that you told me that out of all my brothers, I displayed the greatest ability to lead? Hey, you...you there!" he called to a familiar female onlooker.

"No one ever said that Josem, and no one ever will!" the young woman retorted. She folded her arms across her chest as the crowd erupted into laughter. Emil had sable eyes and long reddish-brown hair. She looked at him flirtatiously, daring him to respond.

"Remind me to openly reject you when all the beautiful virgins of every kingdom are presented before me to be my queen." Josem snapped, causing another wave of laughter to ripple through the crowd.

"Absolutely our prince…" she replied, hands on her hips, "but you would have to remind me to care!" Emil shrugged. The crowd watched her walk away coquettishly.

"Oooohh!" taunted the remnants of the crowd that had stayed long enough to be entertained by the pair's bantering. Josem eagerly followed Emil, displeased with her dismissal. Everyone was accustomed to Josem and Emil's flirtatious teasing. The younger Raiders were especially amused by it. Many of the young men wanted Emil as a wife but they could never compete with Josem's unparalleled quick wit, bravery, roguish ways, boyish good looks, and lineage. Women occasionally dared to seduce Josem's heart away from Emil when she wasn't watching, and he found it entertaining to watch them scurry away when she reappeared. The older

Raiders had grown tired of any romantic advances that didn't lead immediately to marriage.

Josem had wanted to marry Emil since they were children. He proposed to her on her birthday every year when they were children before Surep, her Raider father, moved her and her family to the Southern Outer Lands, but she always ruefully refused. Josem was now a man, but he had never regained the courage to ask her again. Emil was small in stature, but she matched Josem in intelligence, charm, and determination. In conversation it was obvious that Josem had a worthy opponent. He loved her and although she often seemed annoyed with his overwhelming confidence, it was evident that Emil loved him as well.

*****

Basins were brought for Illiam and Nabe to wash away the muck from the journey. After they changed into tunics that Josepher provided for them he began to laugh as he poured wine for them.

"That Josem has a talent to influence a boulder to roll onto its side," he said.

"That's because not even a boulder is as hard as his head!" Nabe teased. He looked over at Illiam. "Are you alright brother?"

"I am very well Nabe. Thank you," Illiam responded.

"I don't know how much your brothers have spoken to you about this…" said Josepher as he continued his quick preparation of food. "But…since you are the eldest among the king's sons and…" Josepher paused. "Well, our people have no king."

"Do they really need one?" Illiam asked unmoved. Josepher looked at Illiam in confusion and then at Nabe with concern.

"Your father left many princes but no one to lead them. Arlan has assumed the position but refuses to take the title. The twins Kasher and Dimos, Lom, Tosh and Roe…"

"Yes, I've already met Tosh and Roe," Illiam said smiling at Nabe.

"Yes, well all of them refused, even Nabe," Josepher responded eager to press the urgency of the situation that they were currently in.

"I don't want it!" Nabe exclaimed, raising his hands in opposition before Josepher could complete his sentence. He didn't want to touch the subject let alone the appointment. Josepher nudged his head toward Nabe as his point was proven.

"Do you see? This leaves us with Josem and Raylen, the two youngest who are barely equipped to rule themselves!"

"I didn't come here to rule," Illiam said plainly.

"Then why else are you here Illiam?" Josepher asked in frustration.

"I'm here to see my family. They need to know that I am alive and I need to tell them about the mercy of the Great One who…"

"Brother!" Josem shouted as he stumbled into the tent with a goblet in his hands. "You have to try this wine. This is the sweetest wine that I've ever tasted," he said thrusting the goblet into Illiam's hand.

"It's also the most intoxicating. I can smell it from here. It has Meraflax," chided Josepher. "One sip of it will inebriate you for days. It is meant for our injured and dying. Our women

61

are the ones who are gifted to cultivate it. Each one has her own effect and it seems Emil has gotten the best of him again!" Josepher laughed. "When will the two of you stop the games and finally marry?" he asked after Josem fell onto the cushions on the floor fast asleep. "It seems now that both Nabe and *I* will have to take you farther north to see Arlan and your mother on the morrow." Nabe looked at Josepher in surprise but Josepher winked at him reassuringly.

"What about Josem?" Illiam asked, handing the goblet to Nabe.

"I'm sure he's already satisfied with whom he came to see," Nabe responded, shaking his head as he poured the remaining contents of the goblet into a small extra-thick wine skin and tied it with a string. He placed it by the belt and daggers that he had removed when he arrived. Josepher returned his attention to Illiam.

"Do you know the history of the Raiders? We only know one way of living. We're a people who know nothing but war. Our training through generations to our sons, and *their* sons, was to track our enemies, strike them, subdue, plunder, and wipe them from the face of the earth. We're taught how to shoot darts from our mouths as soon as we cut our first teeth.

Actually, my boy was barely walking when, unbeknownst to me, he grabbed my blade from its sheath while still in my arms and threw it directly at my neighbor's tent, cutting his arm while he was still inside," he said proudly. Illiam looked over at Nabe for confirmation but he only shook his head and shrugged slightly in response. "This is all we have known my prince." Josepher continued. "And your father, and his father before him and so on have ruled over us not to just keep the order among us, but to keep us unified to prevent the dangers around us from consuming our people."

"Why haven't you and your family moved farther north of the Outer Lands to the Northern Raider Camp like the others?" Illiam asked.

"As I've told you, we're fragmented. Arlan and Mosimer rule over the Raiders in the north. I am the commander of the Raider Clan here. Many of us believe that when Mosimer returned he and the others with him were possessed by the King of the Plains People. Mosimer was the highest ranking among us who escaped that day. We were told that our king was dead, and his heir was taken, but they refused to go back to recover you or to avenge your father's death."

"So, you weren't there that day?" Illiam asked.

"No, but my older brother and general, Urius, was one of the few who survived. He couldn't stop talking about the Good King and his might. From the way he carried on, I thought for a while that he would leave our people and live among the Plains People. He now lives in the Northern Outer Lands in your brother's camp. They're all likeminded," Josepher said mockingly. He placed food on the table in front of them before taking a seat on the cushions beside them.

"Mosimer and the others raised your brothers as though they were their own and taught them all of our ways. They learned quickly and developed skills worthy of your father's throne. Mosimer married your mother. Finally, when Arlan had grown older and strong enough, we assumed that he would avenge his father's death…and yours, if need be, and continue his campaign."

He continued, "Arlan also refused, which made many of us angrier, and the People of the Hills began to rebel against him. Mercenaries and barbarians from the Northern and Southern Valleys came to take advantage of the chaos among our people. Arlan fought with us against them, his skills unmatched. He and Mosimer led us into victory in protecting the People of the Hills. They drove the last of them to the north. After his return, with Mosimer still by his side, Arlan set forth new laws that turned warriors into merchants, tradesmen, and farmers. Our ramparts were converted to gardens, our strongholds to pastures. The princes also learned to live off the land and became guardians among the people."

Illiam listened to Josepher intently. "How did the Raiders remain divided if your battle was so successful?" he asked as his curiosity grew.

"Arlan and Mosimer left the Hills to pursue the last of the enemies that we defeated, and more of our Raider Clan followed them here. Our enemies were defeated, and they left no one alive... or so we thought. Soon after, more of the Raiders left the Hills and occupied this camp. They brought their wives and children with them. Our clan numbers started to grow. The princes were commanded by Arlan to stay behind and to protect the Hills People within the mainland. Then Arlan moved farther north with Mosimer, your mother, and all the Raiders who were witnesses the day you were taken. They've camped dangerously close to the mountainous caverns of fire in which lives tremendous evil. These people that you have seen this evening are the Raider Clan that refused to follow Arlan, Mosimer, and inevitably, my brother farther north. It has been more than fifteen years since I have seen my brother," Josepher concluded.

"So, your arrival won't be the only surprise, Illiam," Nabe said, smiling in an attempt to lighten the conversation.

"But this impending danger is serious, Illiam!" Josepher continued passionately. "This is why we are fragmented and why, after all this time, we are living in tents and keeps instead of mighty strongholds and fortresses. We live like the Nomads to the south and the east. Our darkest nature has been tempted to where some have even abandoned us and fled to our enemies in the northern caverns where those menacing creatures exist. They are forming armies. Probably as we speak. There's a dark feeling. It's as though they are calling to us. Therefore, there must be a king to unite our people and join our lands together." Josepher said with desperation, his deep voice trembling. Illiam sat quietly. He understood why the Raiders wanted a leader but didn't think he was qualified to lead them…Least of all him.

*****

Early the next morning, Josepher led the way along the trail that let farther northeast within the Outer Lands. For now, he decided not to press the matter, but he knew that when they arrived at the northern camp, Illiam would see for himself the dire need to unite the Raider Clan and to fight the impending doom at hand. Illiam and Nabe were on his heels. This time, Illiam had gotten plenty of food and rest for his journey. He was able to match each step that Josepher and Nabe took but was still full of questions. "Did my mother have more children with Mosimer?" he asked Josepher.

"No. Your mother was content with her two sons."

"Two? What do you mean?"

"The king's wives have one thing in common. They are all very stubborn, but your mother is the worst! She knew that she would see you again, and no one could convince her of anything different from the day you were taken. She spoke of you as if you were still alive and still with her."

Did my leaving drive her insane? Illiam felt the pain of guilt rise in him again. *"MURDERER!"* The voice rang out again as the image of his mother appeared in his mind of her going mad and driving everyone away with tattered clothes and a matted braid. At least the few good memories he had left of her included her long, thick, dark brown hair in a braid that he used to liken to silken rope. As a child, he would sneak up behind her and put rocks, sticks, flowers, or any small thing he could find in her braid and then run before she could catch him. The pang of guilt arose faster this time. This was usually a prelude to that insidious voice that plagued him with accusation and condemnation.

"It's funny, she always told us to keep a sharp eye at the gate. Your mother said to treat every stranger as a brother because he very well may be the brother that we lost. We always treated it as a proverb, but now…here you are!" Nabe said, providing a welcome distraction.

Reliable Nabe, Illiam thought as he patted his brother on the shoulder and gave thanks to the Great One for bringing him relief.

*****

The three men traveled the entire day and then camped by the fire in the middle of the vast Outer Lands fields. They ate the fresh meat of a grazing beast that had been separated from its fold. In tracking and killing the beast, Josepher had shown Illiam firsthand the famous Raider skill of crippling prey with precision by shooting it with tiny poison darts with his mouth.

After Josepher blew the deadly darts through the hollow of his fist, it had run away with speed that belied its heft. The darts hit the beast on the front and hind legs of its right side as it ran. As Josepher began to track the animal he saw moss removed in certain places on a series of boulders as if something had brushed against it. Josepher touched the pattern and then looked at Nabe who nodded in understanding.

Josepher quietly squatted to observe the ground. "These tracks are going in circles," he whispered to Illiam as he observed the patterned footprints more closely. Illiam became excited. He and Nabe eagerly followed Josepher along the path of the heavy footprints although the definite direction of the beast's whereabouts was still unclear. Josepher suddenly stopped. He stood in silence for a while and looked into the sky above. This caused Illiam to look up as well.

I wonder what he is looking for, Great One. It's hard to tell if he is tracking a beast or the weather, Illiam thought. He grew hungry at the thought of a belly full of a fresh kill. He hoped that they'd be in front of a fire before they began another day's journey farther into the Outer Lands. Just then, a flock of birds flew away from the place where Josepher was looking.

Ahh! So that is why… Illiam concluded. *He knew a disoriented beast of that size would excite the birds. If they are willing to teach me Great One, please help me to learn well.*

Nabe looked at Illiam. He put his finger to his lips and turned his head in the direction that the birds had fled. After a moment, the three men heard a bellow to the east. They moved toward the cry until they could pick up his scent. The smell of the poison was strong in the air smelling almost as bad as the Bog they had traveled through the day before. Nabe ran ahead to trap the beast and gestured for Illiam to follow. His plan was to barricade it by knotting thin, strong vines together quickly and wrapping them skillfully between the trees with Illiam's assistance. When Nabe was satisfied with his trap he mounted one fist on top of the other, brought them to his mouth, and blew out a loud cry that resembled the cry of a grazing beast. Illiam was so impressed that he wanted to try as well but he came to his senses when he felt the ground rumble as Josepher drove the limping beast frantically toward them.

*****

As they enjoyed their meal that evening, Illiam could no longer contain his excitement.

"You're unbelievable huntsmen! I wouldn't have tried to kill a wild beast that large."

"He was large but young," Josepher said, trying not to show his embarrassment at the compliment. "Any larger and I would have reconsidered it, but with Nabe here I felt confident. Nabe smiled as he used his dagger to poke the slab of meat hanging over the fire.

There was a warmth about Josepher behind the heavy beard and the deep brown eyes hidden under his heavy brow. He had battle-scarred hands and a raven on his arm that matched the one Illiam had noticed on his brother Tosh when they'd met at Josem's home. Nabe always wore his full uniform, but while he traveled with Illiam, he walked around without his hood. Illiam also noticed that Nabe wore leather gloves that exposed his fingers. He guessed that Nabe was skilled with a bow or another weapon of its kind, even though he never carried one. Illiam's curiosity had gotten the best of him.

"It's a unique skill that you have with the darts you spew," Illiam said.

"What darts?" Josepher teased. He reached under his tunic and pulled out a handful of very long, thin, needle-like darts that were flattened at one end and sharp as razors at the other.

"How do you carry so many weapons up your sleeves and under your tunics?"

"We've mastered this and many other things, my prince. We would be honored to teach them to you if you were to become king," Josepher said as he began to eat. Illiam's enthusiasm faded. He didn't want to be king. He wanted a simple life where he could help others who were in real need, which he thought was more than he deserved. He didn't want to help a race of people who sought to regain their power and dominance over the land.

"You mentioned that Mosimer and the other Raiders were possessed by the Good King...What did you mean by that?" Illiam asked, changing the subject.

"Hmph!" Josepher complained. "Good King! What makes him so good? He steals children away to watch their father die. Hmph! He even took you as a trinket to commemorate his victory!"

"You haven't been told? I made a vow to stay," Illiam stated matter-of-factly.

Josepher stopped eating. He lowered the wide, meaty bone of the beast from his lips, looking at Illiam in surprise then at Nabe, and then back at Illiam. Eyes wide, he paused and then raged, "Were you mad boy? Why would a boy who watched his king...no, his father...die...ask to be held captive?"

Illiam tried his best to conceal the rage that had begun to rise inside him as if he were standing on the Plains watching his father take his last breath all over again.

"Someone had to pay for my father's sins, and no one else stepped forward! Actually, no one else should have but me since I am his first born and heir."

"Sins?!" Josepher shouted with a mocking laugh. "What sins? Those people blocked our path to the sea for generations. We were looking for new trade routes and a new source of food. Our nation was multiplying faster than our resources could bear. If it weren't for your father, the Hills People...who are also your and *my* people...would have disappeared from starvation and destitution."

"Were the people of the Hills starving or destitute when my mother's tribe was annihilated by the Great River by his command? What route were they hindering?" Illiam asked with contempt.

"Aye, you are possessed by that demon as well, aren't you? I should have known when we saw your unnatural youth and strange accent that you have been bewitched."

Unmoved, Illiam looked at Josepher. He didn't flinch when he was accused of being beguiled by the Great One or his faithful follower.

"As you have said," he responded, "we are all of one mind." Illiam looked deeply into Josepher's narrowed eyes, his own eyes blazing like the fire that crackled before them. Nabe watched quietly, as he often did, waiting cautiously to see Josepher's reaction to Illiam's admission. His blade was steady in his hand as he slowly carved another piece of meat from the roasted beast.

Josepher took his last bite of meat before tossing the bone and what little was left on it into the fire. He told Illiam, "You should eat and rest. Our journey will conclude on the morrow." He rolled onto his side, pulling the thick beast skin he wore over his shoulder to sleep. Illiam cut another piece of meat from the roasted beast and ate as he stared at the fire in deep thought. Nabe tossed his own bone into the fire and turned onto his side for the night. Surprisingly, the bones sent up a sweet smell as they smoldered until morning.

The Northern Outer Lands

Illiam didn't sleep. He watched the fire die out and the moon greet the sun as they shared opposite ends of the sky like a changing of a guard. Although he tried, he hadn't been able to close his eyes. His conversation with Josepher had struck a nerve and reawakened anger.

Several hours before, his discerning little brother Nabe had awoken abruptly and walked toward the wooded area in search of privacy. He had hardly noticed that Illiam was sitting in the same place he had been before he fell asleep. Josepher had tossed about the entire evening. He even awoke once to see Illiam still sitting by the dwindling fire, mumbled something under his breath, and turned over to the opposite side to sleep.

"Did you sleep well, brother, or not at all? Nabe asked Illiam as he approached.

"The latter, brother," Illiam replied. Nabe stared at Illiam for a moment and then stated plainly, "I figured so. Don't let Josepher get to you. He's a grumpy old man with too many scars and too many traditions to uphold."

"And too many winks of sleep, my young prince! Josepher groaned as he sat up. "If we were still by The Lake That Provides, we could have soaked the flesh before we ate it. We should have at least cut the slab along the middle away from the heart." He groaned again with his heavy accent as he stretched. "We may be immune to the fate of the poison, but not to these effects," he said after a huge yawn.

Nabe walked over and handed him a skin of water. Josepher swallowed three long gulps and wiped away the excess that had spilled onto his beard. "When did you awake?" he asked Illiam with the same contempt as the evening before.

"Yesterday morn," Illiam replied in an accent he knew the Raider commander would recognize. He made no attempt to hide his frustration with Josepher's resentment, but his anger dampened when he saw the fear in Josepher's eyes.

"Those darts should have knocked you down almost as hard as the beast that filled your stomach! Do you mean to tell me that you haven't slept one wink?" Josepher asked in surprise. Illiam shrugged. Somehow, the simple gesture satisfied him but unnerved Josepher.

Great One, I don't know what he is so afraid of, but please show Josepher who's really in control, Illiam said in a silent prayer as Nabe laughed at their harmless dispute and shook his head. Nabe then extended his hand to pull Josepher to his feet.

Josepher stood with a groan and pulled Nabe close to whisper in his ear, "This brother of yours, is he real or are we entertaining a ghost? Nabe laughed again. "I have a feeling that we haven't seen the best part of it yet," he replied as he gathered his things with a sudden gush of excitement and relief. "It won't be too much farther from here, brother. Not even a day's journey." He drew a deep breath and began to walk. Illiam followed.

"Ahh…a new day!" Nabe continued. "The air freezes the farther north we travel. That is why the tunics we were given are lined so heavily. Prepare your mind to move swiftly through the cold. All of our needs will be met when we arrive there."

"I wonder what Josem's doing," Illiam interjected randomly.

"He'll be asleep for at least three days, depending on how much Meraflax he consumed, but once he awakes...do you really want to know how much trouble he's capable of getting into?" Nabe asked.

"Not really, no," Illiam replied with a smile. Still a little groggy from his sleep, Josepher walked behind the men and tried to keep his composure as the two princes continued forward quickly and with ease.

*****

Nabe kept a steady pace. He traveled close enough to remain in Josepher's sight but far enough ahead to talk privately with Illiam. "Although the Raiders are boastful, they weren't born this way, they were bred. They were like any other conquered nation of people who were forced into war by our ancestors among the Hills People, but their clan excelled at it. I once heard Mosimer admit that they were, "Soaked in the tradition of war and then wrung out into battle," Nabe recalled. "He said that they naturally don't know any other way and that only the supernatural would have a chance at changing their minds. He called his people loyal, stubborn, and incredibly superstitious, a bad combination when they're allied with the wrong kind of leader," he added. "They kept their promise to the Good King, and from that day...you know, the day you and Father were gone, they raised us well. We wanted for nothing."

"From the day that Father and I were gone, as you say, the Good King raised *me* also, and *I* wanted for nothing. Instead of gratitude for his kindness, all I've heard throughout the hills is contempt and bitterness toward him." Illiam complained. "Is there anyone among the Hills People who knows how to be grateful? Do they know what mercy is? Illiam stopped and drew a deep breath. He looked around, trying as best he could to regain his composure.

"Soon brother..." Nabe said in a low calm voice. "We'll be there soon to see those who may understand you." He looked back to see Josepher walking farther behind than he expected and called out, "Are you well old man?" Josepher looked up and waved his hand dismissing Nabe's harmless teasing.

"The air is strange today," he called back. Nabe waited for him to catch up. "I don't know if you've noticed but it should be much colder now that we've reached this point. Instead, I want to remove my tunic," said Josepher. He removed the large beast skin that he had used as a covering the night before and then wiped the sweat from his brow.

"It is very strange," Nabe replied.

"Then keep your eyes open men. There may be a demon nearby," Josepher said. He searched the sky as he had when he was tracking their meal the day before. Creatures flew overhead, but this time in a hovering pattern. They were large scavenger beasts that screeched violently as they circled above. The men moved forward as quickly as they could in search of something to hide behind until they could see what was wrong. They found a crevice in the earth that was deep enough for them to crawl into. As they waited, watched, and listened, Illiam's hands began to shake uncontrollably. He tried to control his fear of the unexpected, but he had heard of the Catacombs beyond the Hills and feared that the demon Josepher was referring to might be one of their scouts or worse. He reached for his small blade and tried to steady it in his hand by grasping his wrist with his other hand.

Great One, we need you. Please help us! Illiam prayed. After a short while, the beasts dispersed toward the north as if something had scared them, although nothing was in sight.

81

"Take heart, young princes. We won't be anyone's meal today," Josepher announced. "It seems that whatever was near us to influence those wretched flying beasts has gone." The three men cautiously left the crevice but moved about back to back to cover themselves from all angles. It was the first time since leaving the land of the Plains People that Illiam longed for the Good King's confidence and protection.

The Dark Voice

Astrong cold wind began to blow as the three men reached a high bridge over a deep and wide valley.

"The camp is just over this bridge and the chill is becoming for this altitude and season," Josepher said. Illiam's teeth began to chatter. He found that instead of fearing an unseen demon or flesh eating, flying beasts he was experiencing an uncontrollable rage rise in him.

"If your father was a good king, your family wouldn't have moved this close to the catacombs. They would have lived peacefully among the Hills, but he's dead, and his curse still follows you!" the Dark Voice whispered fiercely. Nabe saw Illiam's brows furrow and directed him to walk in front of him so that he could cross the

bridge. The wide planked bridge swung and bounced, making it nearly impossible to move forward. The metal handrails creaked unnervingly. The howling of the wind was so loud, and the force was incredibly violent as it whipped around them, causing the men to desperately grasp for the ropes that were intertwined between the steel links along the sides.

"This isn't an ordinary wind! Keep moving Illiam!" Nabe shouted to his brother who had suddenly stopped in front of him to shield his eyes. Illiam pushed against the wind toward the end of the bridge. He peeked below his sleeve as best he could to see where he could find purchase on the widely spaced planks beneath.

When the men finally reached the end of the bridge a road appeared past two gargantuan rocks on each side. The gale subsided just as quickly and unexpectedly as it had arrived, leaving the air cold but bearable. Nabe readjusted the sack of water, dried meat, and Meraflax that he had strapped over his chest, and Josepher removed the hood of beast skin that he used to cover himself against the cold winds.

"Is everyone well?" Josepher asked, looking disheveled.

"I wish for our sake that *you* could have gone ahead and shielded us from the event we just endured. Besides your hair and your faithful scowl, you look almost untouched," Nabe said.

"Well, you wanted to lead, and I thought it was very well time that one of you did!" Josepher exclaimed defensively. The princes looked at one another in disbelief at Josepher's relentless expectations.

Something strange caught Illiam's eye as he glanced back at the foot of the bridge. Peering more closely he saw what looked like a man with the face of a beast and a long, thick tail. It was pacing as if something was preventing it from crossing the bridge. Illiam's lips turned white and his hands grew cold as ice, but when he blinked again, the image was gone. Nabe studied his brother silently. He wanted to ask, but instead he grabbed Illiam by the arm and followed Josepher. We're almost there," he whispered softly.

The Unlikely Visitor

The men turned off the short road toward the camp's southern perimeter and were met by a closed gate. The two pairs of guards on each side wore white tunics with white fur hides around their legs, arms, hands, and necks. When they saw Nabe and Josepher with a guest, they extended a Raider salute then opened the gates without question.

"What misery has caused you to come this far north into the Outer Lands to see the bewitched, Josepher Southern Raider?" Mosimer asked with a scowl. He stood tall with his arms folded across his broad chest and a huge white furry hide draped across one shoulder. As Josepher approached other Raiders from the northern camp gathered curious to see whom Mosimer was addressing with such distaste.

A few young men ran to Josepher, eyes wide. "Uncle Josepher!" one of his nephews among them cried out as he embraced him. "It's been a long time. I've missed you!"

"And I you!" Josepher replied with a gleam in his eye. "Aye, you're a man now! You may want to leave this miserable place and join your kin in the south!"

"You know my father would never allow it," his nephew responded with a smile. "Besides, more men are needed here since…" His words trailed off as he looked at the other young men around him. "Anyway, what brings *you* here?" he asked in an attempt to lighten the mood.

"That's what *I'll* be asking him, boy!" came a deep voice that sounded a lot like Josepher's. There beside Mosimer stood an equally large man with a heavy brow and a thick graying beard.

"My dear brother Urius!" Josepher yelled out.

"I thought we agreed to defend our lands in our own way. What brings you here now?" Urius asked with skepticism.

87

"I came to bring you a gift!" Josepher replied. Just then, Nabe and Illiam stepped forward. Josepher smiled smugly and moved to the side to allow the men to see the princes.

"Nabe?" Mosimer asked. "Is that you young prince? It has been too long since I've returned to visit you and your brothers." He bowed to Nabe who grabbed and embraced him. Mosimer's cheeks reddened with sudden embarrassment. He cleared his throat and asked, "And who did you bring? Don't tell me this is Josem."

"No Mosimer. Josem is less reserved if you can remember," Nabe replied.

"Raylen then?" There are so many of you that I can hardly tell you apart, especially now that you have all grown. Arlan, told us about the wonderful deeds of our princes in our main country."

"We left Josem in the southern camp, and Raylen, as far as I know, is still at home in the Hills with Isha Ptrina living as quietly as possible," Nabe said, hoping that Mosimer and the others would be able to discern for themselves who was in their midst.

"Come closer, brother," Nabe insisted to Illiam as Josepher stood to the side chuckling to himself. The crowd grew as Mosimer and Urius became more confused. Illiam waited silently. As Mosimer moved closer to peer into his eyes his face revealed that he remembered the prince who stood before him.

"My God, Hilda!" Mosimer cried as he turned and tore through the crowd toward his tent. The crowd watched in confusion. Who was this stranger who could cause Mosimer, Commander of the Northern Raider Clan, to react in such a way?

"What are you up to, Josepher?" Urius asked furiously.

"I was hoping to bring you a king, Urius," Josepher replied.

"From what womb was he birthed?" called one voice from the crowd. "Yes, which queen bore him?" cried out another. Nabe stood in front of Illiam to shield him from their protests as he witnessed the anger that began to form on their faces.

Still shaken by the creature he had seen at the bridge, Illiam became disoriented by the noise of the crowd and the Dark Voice that had begun to creep back into his consciousness. *"Murderers! You saw your fate at the bridge. You don't deserve peace.*

Now that you are all together you will all die! Murderers!" The haunting voice entranced him. Josepher noticed the crowd's hostility was growing as some began to pick up stones and form flanks around the princes.

After someone shouted, "This is Sorcery!" Josepher moved into the center of the crowd and stood by the two princes. "The northern clan is not as welcoming as we are in the south, are they, Nabe? Perhaps the air is too thin up here," Josepher said mockingly. His tall and wide build blocked Illiam completely as he and Nabe stood their ground.

"He is no prince!" Another voice cried out.

"Aye, but he is indeed. He is Illiam!" Josepher proclaimed. He stood as if daring anyone to try to pass him. The noise suddenly quieted to a murmur.

"Cease!" A commanding voice cut through the crowd. It was Arlan. He walked on one side of his mother while Mosimer walked on the other. The people bowed and shifted allowing them to pass. Arlan had brown eyes, cropped hair, and a short dark beard. He wore a white Raider tunic with a gold braided belt at his waist. Hilda, his mother, wore a similar garment in the fashion of the women of the Hills but instead of silk she wrapped a golden woolen cord around her waist, and white fur hides around her shoulders and feet to withstand the cold. A long dark braid draped over her shoulder. Her hand rested in the bend of Arlan's arm, and she stood tall and strong as they approached the core of all the confusion.

"Josepher, what brings *you* here?" Arlan asked curiously.

"I wanted to see if I could still cause a scene," Josepher replied.

"It seems that you have succeeded," Arlan said with concern.

"I never had a doubt my prince," Josepher continued with a bow. "Isha Hilda, you look well."

"As do you Josepher…and Nabe you've come too? How are your mother and brothers? Is everything all right in the south?" Hilda asked. Even with his head pounding in torment at the sound of her voice Illiam moved forward between his two protectors and stood in front of his mother and brother for the first time since he was a boy.

Hilda recognized him immediately. She froze and would have fallen to the ground if Mosimer hadn't been near enough

91

to catch her. "ILLIAM!" she cried as she shook and wept. She reached for him and embraced him tightly. Arlan staggered back and tears welled in his eyes when he heard his brother's name. The crowd stood in shock. Illiam tried his best to take in the moment but he found it too difficult to focus. The Dark Voice screamed louder as his mother wept in his arms. Everything began to spin around him as fear gripped him and wouldn't let go. He embraced his mother until his legs gave out and he fell to the ground almost taking her with him.

"What is it?" she screamed in panic. "What is it my son?" Josepher, what's happening?"

"I don't know Milady Hilda! He was fine all this time!" Josepher exclaimed. "Indeed, he never slept though. Even after tasting poison from the flesh of our kill last eve, he hasn't closed his eyes since the morn on yesterday. Perhaps he isn't immune to the poison. Perhaps it has doomed him instead."

Arlan ran to Illiam and put his head to his chest. "His heart is racing! Why is it racing? Everyone get back! Give him room!" he shouted.

"Foolishness!" screamed Hilda frantically. "My son did not come all this way to die!" Illiam could see the distress on all of their faces. He saw them scrambling around him through partially closed eyes, but he couldn't hear a word they were saying. The only words he heard over and over again were, *"Murderers! The time has come! There is no escape! Judgment has come!"*

Nabe who had been frozen in shock quickened. He pressed through the crowd and jostled Arlan aside to kneel beside Illiam. He turned Illiam's head toward him, noting that his eyes were barely opened, and he couldn't move.

"He is being tormented, Arlan," Nabe said in a voice for only Arlan to hear. He raised the skin of Meraflax that he carried with him and shook it in front of Illiam's face hoping Illiam would recognize it and then poured a few drops into his mouth. "Rest brother; just rest." Illiam heard him murmur as his eyes closed and he drifted off to sleep.

"Quickly, carry him to my tent. He's beginning to grow pale from the cold," Arlan commanded. Raider soldiers ran to move Illiam as quickly and as gently as possible to Arlan's tent. Arlan walked with Nabe and patted him on the shoulder. They embraced and then followed the men who carried Illiam.

"What did you mean when you said that he's being tormented?" Arlan finally asked when they arrived at the tent.

"I've seen that look on him before," Nabe answered. "It appeared when we were with the southern clan as well. He lost focus and looked about as if something was calling him. He fights it, but something haunts him."

"Ahh! We are too close to the Catacombs!" Arlan exclaimed. "We've lost many men, women and now children to the Dark Voice!" he said pacing as he ran his hand over his cropped dark hair.

"The Dark Voice?" Nabe asked, confused.

"It calls to us, but we never know who or when until it's too late," Arlan confessed. "The closer we get, the more powerful it becomes."

"Do you really think the Catacombs are the cause of this?" Nabe asked.

"Why do you ask? Speak your mind freely, Nabe."

"It just crossed my mind that Illiam is one of us by birth but not by culture, yet he is tormented. What could bring him so much misery that the Dark Voice would draw him? What has he seen and what does he know? I believe there is more to it than what we see, brother," Nabe concluded. "If you'll allow me to stay with him for now, you can go comfort your mother while I prepare him for his long rest. You can bring her to him when I've made him ready."

Arlan looked at Nabe with pride as he smiled and patted his shoulder again. Reassured Arlan asked, "Why haven't we asked for your council before?" Nabe shrugged and smiled as he began to unstrap Illiam's sandals. Arlan laid a freshly cleaned tunic on the cushion beside him before he left.

The Wait

Arlan walked across the camp to his mother's tent to comfort her. Mosimer held her tightly as she grieved for her son. When she saw Arlan she hastened to question him.

"Arlan, how is he?" Hilda asked frantically as she left Mosimer's arms.

"He is resting, and it seems that the only one qualified to be with him at this moment is Nabe," Arlan reassured her.

"He was always peculiar... but special, even as a boy," Mosimer recalled.

"When can I see him?" his mother asked refusing to waste any time.

"Soon mother," he replied. "From the smell of it, it seems that he will be under the influence of the small dose of Meraflax that Nabe gave him for a few days. He knew that the tonic would calm him."

"Calm him? Calm him from what, Arlan?" Hilda asked unnerved. "What has happened to him? She turned to Josepher who had just consumed his second serving of bread, cheese, and mixed wine.

"Milady, as I have said before…I don't know," Josepher replied with a slight slur and a belch.

"Arlan, go to the infirmary and bring my satchel of Meraflax," said Hilda in disgust. "I will give this fool something to quench his thirst indeed." Arlan smiled shaking his head knowing that his mother had never mastered the art of cultivating the tonic to be used for anything less than sudden death, unlike the native Raider women who had learned its medicinal uses from childhood.

"Now Hilda," Mosimer scolded gently. "Your visions have come true and your prayers have been answered. Miraculously you have both of your sons with you. One is standing before you and the other is resting in our care, so that he is able to heal. He has been brought back to us by the Great One and as you have already said, he will not die. There must be a greater purpose that we're unaware of …I am sure of it. We must be patient, even with Josepher. So please my dear, try not to kill him."

Mosimer rubbed her shoulders to ease her tension. She calmed as Arlan laughed. "He's right Mother, the Great One still has a purpose for Josepher too. He did help bring Illiam to us."

A few minutes later Hilda's youngest attendant entered the tent with a bow.

"Isha Hilda and Commander Mosimer…" she stopped midsentence bowing to acknowledge Arlan's presence. "And good evening our prince. General Urius desires to enter to retrieve Commander Josepher."

"He may enter," Isha Hilda responded. Urius bowed as he entered the tent.

"I can smell his arrogance from here. I came to take my brother off your hands. This act alone should completely destroy any doubt of how gracious I really am," he announced as he walked over to a sleeping Josepher. He jostled him awake and helped him to his feet. "Come along, you braggart," he said as he helped support the weight of his drunken and exhausted brother. "I have a tent filled with a wife and children who actually *want* to see you."

Josepher leaned on his brother and staggered out of the tent. Arlan followed them and said to Urius, "Take care and find out what you can from Josepher about their journey. Nabe mentioned the Dark Voice and gave Illiam Meraflax to help him somehow overcome it. It will at least give us more time to ask the Great One for direction. We will go to Nabe shortly to learn more. I will inform you of what we discover."

"I will do as you ask, my prince," Urius replied. "Now if you don't mind, this old man is terribly heavy." Arlan immediately propped himself under Josepher's free arm with the intention of helping Urius bring him to his tent but he was greeted and relieved of his kind gesture by a few Raider men who were also Urius's three older sons. Arlan ran back to escort his mother to see Illiam who was then sleeping peacefully on a bed of cushions, pillows and soft white linen and skins. "Oh, Great One!" Hilda sighed rubbing his head as he slept. "You've protected our children all of this time. Don't let any of them be lost."

*****

The next day Josepher awoke on an unfamiliar pallet of sleeping mats. "Where am I?" he asked, looking up to see two little children standing over him and giggling. "Who are you?" he asked with squinted eyes.

The first, a little girl, handed him a jug of water. "Alyssa, uncle!" she said scolding him for not knowing who she was with her hands planted firmly on her hips.

The other was a boy who said, "I'm Edenmer, uncle. Did you know that you snore when you sleep?"

"Yes, and you smell too!" Alyssa added, holding her nose.

"Aren't you two the perfect welcoming committee?" Josepher said wryly before he swallowed down the fresh cold water that Alyssa gave him.

"Father told us that we were to send you to him when you were finally awake, and now you are!" declared Edenmer.

"Yes, finally!" exclaimed his sister anxiously.

"Where is your father now?" Josepher asked.

"He said to meet him at the tent of Commander Mosimer," Edenmer said.

"Do you know where that is?" Alyssa asked.

"I'll figure it out," Josepher replied as he struggled to stand to his feet. His audience giggled even harder. "Are you twins?" he asked.

"Uncle, we're not twins. I'm older than she is!" Edenmer exclaimed.

"You know that I'm your uncle?" he asked amazed.

"Aye, Father says that you are the youngest, but he is the wisest," Edenmer replied.

"Uncle you should really come around more. You don't know anything," Alyssa scolded.

Josepher laughed. "Aye, you really are my brother's children," he said as he made his way out of the tent into the daylight. Squinting, stretching, and scratching he peered around the camp for a tent that looked like something fit for a Raider commander and worthy husband to a queen like Hilda. He saw men coming in and out of a large tent that looked like the one he had entered the evening before. Fellow Raiders saluted him as he walked toward it. He opened the tent and entered to see two women treating a man with an injured leg.

"What is this?" Josepher asked in shock. "Commander Josepher?" One woman asked in surprise as the two women stood abruptly and the patient screamed in pain. "This is the infirmary!"

"I see! Obviously!" he said embarrassed and hung over.

"Where did you want to go?" the other woman asked.

"Mosimer...I'm looking for the tent of Mosimer," he said, distracted by the patient's outcry of pain as his head pounded from the mixed wine he drank the night before.

"Oh yes, it is on the other side of the camp. I can show you if you'd like," she said eager to help.

"No, No! I'll figure it out. Just attend to his wound. He sounds like he's dying," he said.

He exited the tent and walked towards the other side of the camp leaving the puzzled women in his wake.

"It took you long enough! If you can't drink wine and fight a battle within the hour, then you shouldn't drink!" Urius scolded. Josepher winced and held his head.

"Well, your twins gave terrible directions," Josepher replied sarcastically. Urius laughed. 'They don't like to be called twins. I'm sure they gave you an ear full. Here, sit and eat," he offered as Josepher took a seat. He could do no more than drink the warm, sweet ale placed before him.

"You know, you're very ungrateful," Josepher complained. "I brought you the nation's missing prince and possible future king to unite our clans and you didn't even say thank you!"

"Aye, but you brought him back crazy...and near death might I add!" Urius replied.

"It's no thanks to that Good King," Josepher accused in self-defense.

"If not for the Good King you'd be the crazy one talking to a ghost, because I'd be dead." Josepher froze at the cold reality of his brother's words.

"Aww, I don't believe in ghosts," he said decidedly. "That demon and his magic have all of you fooled. Bring swords and flying razors to the fight and see if he bleeds like any other man."

"We did, little brother. We did and we lost…and won all in the same day," Urius responded. "Swords, razors, darts and spears. Warring beasts and flying beasts. No poisons or elixirs will work in this kind of war Josepher. Don't deceive yourself. You have never seen what I've seen, and I hope that you never have to, except to give the Great One praise."

"Aww, there's no getting through to you. Have you considered your family? What kind of man would move his household to live this close to the catacombs, knowing that they could be taken at any time by monsters?" Josepher asked critically.

"A man who has learned that who is for him is greater than who's against him. Don't think that you're safe where you are. There will come a time when you'll have to choose a side. If that miserable threat shows itself at your door, then what real power will be on *your* side, Josepher?" Urius replied resolutely.

Josepher scowled and continued to drink without another word.

In Search of the Prophet

While in Arlan's tent Mosimer whispered, "As a precaution we may have to ask *him* to come."

Arlan considered Mosimer's suggestion. "Do you think he would?"

"If you're referring to the Good King…for Illiam I believe he would," Nabe interjected having overheard the conversation. "Illiam cares for him the way we care for the Raider Clan. They have a bond."

"Then send a band of men to the People of the Plains and humbly request that the Good King help Illiam. Send Josepher with them and tell him to make sure the southern clan does not provoke him. This is my request," Arlan commanded.

"Yes, my prince," replied Mosimer. "I will escort Josepher and the men myself." He kissed Hilda on her forehead and turned to leave.

"Take care!" Nabe warned. "Illiam saw something at the bridge that terrified him after we crossed over. Something was indeed following us, but when I looked to see what it was, nothing was there."

"It could be a scout, Mosimer. Gather all the intercessors to the bridge to pray before you cross. I will meet with you to see you off," Arlan instructed. Mosimer bowed his head in response and quickly exited the tent.

*****

As promised, Nabe refused to leave his brother's side. For two days he had attended to Illiam's needs attentively, accepting support only from Arlan or Isha Hilda.

"You should rest, Nabe," Arlan said looking into his brother's tired eyes.

"I will rest, but if he stirs, I will tend to him. I just..." Nabe paused.

"Nabe, I told you before that your thoughts are an asset to us. Speak freely," Arlan reminded him.

Nabe was accustomed to his opinion being disregarded as nagging or unnecessary. He had learned to keep most of his thoughts to himself because even his smallest thoughts overwhelmed everyone.

Arlan regretted not realizing sooner that Nabe might have the gift of wisdom and discernment from the Great One. He wasn't sure if Nabe even believed. Now, he wanted Nabe to say everything that was on his mind no matter how small it was.

"I'm just hoping that when he wakes, he'll win the battle over his mind. I just want to make sure to be here the moment he does," Nabe disclosed.

"You have a lot of faith Nabe. You've grown close to him in this short time haven't you?"

"There are many mysteries within our eldest brother, Arlan. For the first time ever, I am excited for our future and for his," Nabe said. He wrung out a cool damp cloth in a basin and placed it gently on Illiam's sweating forehead. "He should be awake in a day or so. If you don't mind, I'd like to rest a little now. Could you provide for him until I wake?" He passed the basin to Arlan.

"It would be my pleasure. Rest well," Arlan replied. Nabe loosened his sandals and spread himself out beside Illiam on a cushioned bed that had been prepared for him. He was asleep within seconds.

"So far you have given us Illiam and greater insight into one of my younger brothers. What more could there be, Great One?" Arlan asked. He removed the cloth from Illiam's forehead, dampened it, wrung it out and then positioned it again over his brother's brow.

*****

For three days, Illiam had slept where the Dark Voice couldn't find him. In a dream he saw himself back on the plains with the Good King. He remembered how the Good King had touched his shoulder and said, "There is one last thing I must do before we part, Illiam." In the dream, the Good King had touched his chest causing Illiam's skin to become hardened like the ground beneath his feet. Illiam's body stirred in his sleep as Arlan rested his hand on his forehead.

"I'm here, brother," Arlan said. He began to pray. "Please lead him through this. We can't take losing him again. Please have mercy on us."

*****

A few hours later, Illiam stilled as he began to dream again. He recalled hearing the Good King's words back on the plains, "I impart to you what the Great One gave to me. You and I are now of one mind." Illiam's hardened body softened into putty. He lost the form of a man and sank to the earth like mud.

The Good King squatted beside him, "Without the Great One, like your state now…we can do nothing, but if you trust and follow him there will be no limit to what he can do in and through you. He heard you when you asked to be his forever, but even now you are consumed by guilt and unforgiveness. You have never released your father's deeds from your heart, and bitterness has grown there. The miserable will use that against you. Turn from your hate, turn from your anger, turn to the Great One and forgive your father. Then forgive yourself because you are free to live without shame." The Good King stood. "The reign of fear ended when your father died," the king continued. "All curses on your family have now been broken. The hope of your nation will begin with you. If you do this, fear will no longer imprison you but will flee from you instead. If you don't, you will live out your days as you are right now, and you and your descendants will live and die under your enemies' feet. What, Illiam, do you say to these things?"

In his dream, Illiam's unformed body rippled on the ground before the Good King. As the dream ended his sleeping body shivered slightly before Arlan. Arlan decided to wake Nabe.

"What happened?" Nabe asked, stumbling groggily to his feet and making his way to Illiam's side.

"I wanted you to get as much rest as possible, but he's been stiffening and shivering for hours now," Arlan exclaimed in frustration. "Should we send for one of the women to concoct something that will wake him? I don't know what else to do!"

"This dose of Meraflax came from Josem's Emil. I'm afraid she's the only one who would know all the ingredients within it."

Illiam quietly huffed and shifted as he struggled to open his eyes.

"Wait! The Meraflax is wearing off! He'll be awake soon. If I were to pray to your 'Great One' right now," Nabe said with excitement, "I would pray that when he wakes, he'll be even stronger and better than he was before."

Nabe removed the cloth from Illiam's forehead and put his ear to his chest to check the sound of his heart. He was encouraged that Illiam's heartbeat was steady and saw that he began taking slow calm breaths. He happily looked at Arlan again.

"Then I will pray for both. That you seek the help of the Great One and find that Illiam is even more than he was before," Arlan replied. He studied his younger brother with joy in his heart.

"If my prayer is fulfilled, then seeking him further would be my pleasure," Nabe said with a smile on his tired face.

The men watched as Illiam slowly stretched a few times. They removed his sweaty tunic and replaced it with a fresh clean one. Arlan ran to wake Hilda as soon as the sun rose and Illiam turned over for the first time. His eyes opened and closed as his mother gently massaged his arms and hands that had been still for days. She also used oils and salves to soften his rigid muscles and stimulate his senses.

Mosimer was still on his quest to seek the help of the Good King. Although Illiam's family could not understand what might happen to him, they knew that the Good King's aid was imperative. They would receive no word when Mosimer reached the Southern Raider Clan, or the Hills safely-or at all. The journey to the land of the Plains People should take just a little more than two days on the backs of their swift warring beasts. Mosimer would find a way when, or if, he could.

*****

By noon that day Illiam was finally awake. His mother left his side only long enough to prepare a meal for him and returned with more food than he could eat. She insisted on feeding him as if he were a child.

"Oh Mother, he was ill not a newborn," Arlan complained as he watched on in embarrassment for him.

"Shh! He is to me," she replied, wiping his mouth with the hem of the sash she wore around her waist. Illiam received each bite without complaint dismissing Arlan's words with a wave of his hand.

"It seems that you are alone in this, Arlan," Nabe teased. "He missed his mother as much as she missed him."

Arlan frowned and suggested, "Let's not tell anyone about this." Illiam was laughing so hard at the scene that he and his mother must have made in front of Arlan and Nabe that it was all he could do not to spit out his food.

After Illiam was full and alert he spoke about his dream in a faint voice. It was his first time having an audience that listened to him speak about the Great One and the Good King favorably and without interruption.

"Illiam, you never told us…did you choose to forgive father?" Arlan asked curiously. Suddenly, all attention was on Illiam. He swallowed hard.

"It is true that I hated Father for what he did to you, Mother, and to your people," he said to Hilda. "I've resented that I was feared by others because of the atrocities he left in his wake and because his greed became his legacy for us to carry on. I especially despised that we had to watch him die as me and my brothers, who were mere children, were charged to avenge him after he was found guilty and judged for his sins.

113

Even until his last breath he was unrepentant." Illiam paused as he looked at his brothers.

"It is also true that I was afraid all this time that I would never escape his fate as his heir. Therefore, I decided to take the punishment that he was too much of a coward to receive for the lives he destroyed. All these years I've worked and met the People of the Plains' every expectation as a slave to fulfill my oath. Once it was fulfilled, I was free to do as I pleased but I didn't feel worthy of it." Hilda held his hand and began to cry softly. "No matter what I did I was feared because I was still the son of the King of the Hills People…a murderer, but I was counted with the innocent by the mercy of the Great One. The Good King befriended me and allowed me to sit with him in council. Now that I think of it, I was too self-condemning to understand how much he thought of me." All in the tent were silent as they waited patiently for his next words.

"As in my dream, my weakness condemned me. I would repeatedly hear all my fears. It became deafening until it eventually paralyzed me because I didn't know there was a way out." Illiam looked at Arlan, "Arlan, I forgive Father and I hope that all of you will do the same."

Arlan walked over and gripped his eldest brother's hand. "If you can, brother, then I will also."

Hilda wiped her eyes and said, "I will try." Everyone looked at her, surprised by her confession. "It is very difficult for me to forget all the death and misery that he has caused everyone that I've loved even until now, but for the Great One and to grow closer to him, I will eagerly seek to release your father. I need to seek forgiveness as well for holding on to bitterness toward him for so long."

Hilda kissed and embraced her two sons. Nabe stayed long enough to watch the three comfort one another and the tears flow between them. He decided to strap on his sandals and grab the last of Illiam's old tunics and linens to wash them. Arlan followed him into the daylight.

"Nabe, where are you going? You don't have to clean them. I will ask someone to attend to his things." At Arlan's gesture attendants hurried over to take the tunics from his hands. Nabe squinted in the early afternoon sun and then turned to Arlan, his eyes brimming with tears.

"I prayed, Arlan. I appealed to your 'Great One'. Is it too soon for me to hope? I think that my prayers have been answered." Nabe wiped his eyes as his tears continued to flow. Arlan smiled and embraced him as they walked, eager to hear everything that was on his younger brother's mind.

*****

Three days passed before Mosimer made it safely across the bridge with his men on their warring beasts and Josepher by his side. Josepher looked around cautiously, recalling the unusual change in the atmosphere when they had arrived at the northern camp just a few days before. He didn't say a word about it to Mosimer as they traveled swiftly back to the Southern Raider Camp. The pace of the warring beasts exceeded any progress they would have made on foot. They had reached the camp before evening. Josepher had decided not to use the beasts on their first journey because he wanted to take some time to persuade Illiam to take his rightful place as king, an attempt he considered a failure in the end. As they entered the camp Southern Raiders gathered around Mosimer and greeted him warmly in surprise. Josepher looked for Josem to tell him about all that had occurred on their journey.

"So, you're on your way to the Plains People now?" Josem asked with wide eyes.

"I'm not, but Mosimer and his men are," Josepher replied. "Arlan wants Mosimer to ask their king, who held your brother captive, to journey to the north and save your brother who is sick from whatever it is in the world that ails him. How do we know it wasn't *him* who caused our prince to fall? Why they would call on a demon to relieve someone else's demons is beyond comprehension?" Josepher complained.

"That's enough, Josepher. We'll handle it from here. My men and I will require no more from you but your cooperation when the Good King passes through your camp. Do we have it?" Mosimer asked with all the authority of his rank as Chief Commander among the Raider Clan. Against Urius's better judgment Mosimer had designated Josepher the Commander of the Southern Raider Clan when they were split. Josepher was one of the first to rebel against their conviction and newfound faith in the Great One among the Plains People and their irrepressible king.

"Aye, you'll have it, but we have been divided over this matter long enough," Josepher replied.

"On *that* I agree entirely, Commander."

The clouds rolled and lightening flashed. "Hurry, it is about to rain," urged Josepher. "Let's tie in and refresh your beasts until it subsides. You can set off again once you have eaten and rested." The men dismounted their beasts and were ushered into Josepher's tent.

"Yes, and I'll come with you," Josem replied as though he had been invited. He left no room for argument. Josepher looked at him curiously. He had always believed that Josem's opinion of the one who had murdered his father and held his brother captive was the same as his. "And...I'll ride the beast that Josepher rode on in his stead so don't remove his shackles," Josem added to the keeper of the beasts, not noticing Josepher's gaze of betrayal.

Mosimer smiled. "Splendid idea! Please do as he asked. We will set out as soon as the storm passes."

******

It had rained the entire evening and into the following day without a hint of stopping. The heavy rain caused the lake to rise and triggered mud slides throughout the land. Men were digging trenches around the perimeter of the camp. It became harder to control their beasts against the sound of thunder and the relentless flashes of lightning. Children could be heard screaming in their small wooden homes and the tents covered with beast hides. Their livestock howled and bellowed in response to the strong winds that rocked the walls of their shelters.

"This is unusual," Josepher mused as the band of men waited quietly in his tent. He swallowed another swig of mixed wine from the skin he had brought back from the Northern Raider Camp.

"Nothing has been usual since we met the Good King," Mosimer replied.

"No...I mean like the bridge... This is unusual like when we crossed the bridge! There was wind but no rain, but if it had rained, I believe it would have been like this," Josepher added.

"What happened on the bridge?" Josem asked.

"Your brother Illiam fell ill after we'd crossed. A demon we couldn't see pursued us with flying scavenger beasts. An unbearably cold strange wind all but pushed us off it," he continued slurring his words. "When we entered the camp, he fell and Nabe gave him a drip of Emil's Meraflax to settle him. He hasn't woken and I'm not sure if he ever will."

"Why didn't you tell us this before?" Mosimer asked, Josem's eyes opened wide with fear. He looked to Mosimer for more clarity.

"What does he mean hasn't woken or never will?" he asked anxiously.

"Calm yourself, Josem," Mosimer said with the deep calming timber he used so often to comfort his queen and everyone around him. "Josepher believes that Illiam was poisoned from the meat of a kill they ate the eve beforehand. He and Nabe slept heavily through it, but Illiam not at all. He collapsed in his mother's arms soon after they reunited. We have faith that he will awaken but our journey is just a precaution."

"Then we must move! Why did we sit here so long in fear of this rain and wind if my brother could be dying?" Josem snapped. He rose angrily.

"This storm is dangerous, Josem. We take a great risk of getting hurt or worse if we try to travel in it. You know very well how unforgiving the Hills can be with even less wind and rain," Mosimer stated.

"Traveling the Hills away from the Outer Lands is perilous in stormy circumstances but traveling down them with large and temperamental warring beasts multiplies the risk," Josepher added.

"We'll continue to pray for the rain to cease so we can continue our journey safely. In the meantime, rest yourself, my young prince. I believe waiting will be for the best," Mosimer requested.

"I know nothing about prayer, Mosimer! All I know is that my brother is ill and needs help! Do I have to go alone?" Josem exclaimed. Mosimer looked into Josem's eyes and saw that the young prince had matured noticeably since he had seen him last. He knew that the only way to stop him would be to tie him down. Mosimer stood.

"Men, I believe our young prince has just given his first order. Prepare yourselves for the journey immediately." As the men rose to their feet Josem walked out of the tent and into the howling winds. Rain saturated the entrance of the tent.

One by one the men followed him until Josepher was left alone with Mosimer.

"The Great One is in full command. You'll see my friend. It will all work out," Mosimer said before striding out of the tent and into the maelstrom. Josepher watched him with heavy eyes but said nothing.

*****

Cold driving rain stung the men as they waited mounted on their beasts for the command to move forward. It ran from their heads and soaked them to the skin, but they endured it in hopes they would find the Good King in time to help Illiam.

"Young prince, are you ready to take responsibility not only for your life but for the lives of the men you lead today?" Mosimer asked. Josem nodded resolutely, and they set their course to travel south. *May you help us*, he prayed as he followed.

Neither the rains nor the winds took mercy on the men. Their beasts' eyes were hooded so they could see only what was in front of them. The large heavy shackles on their legs made it easier for them to plant their wide clawed hooves in the earth to resist the strong winds. The cold heavy rain bounced off their thick hides. Covered in thick beast skins and hoods the men rode cautiously through the mud and mire. Mosimer prayed quietly, *"Our Great One, please hear my plea as we voyage at this treacherous time to find your prophet. We have little strength, but we are willing to give our lives to the cause. Help Josem to see his purpose as well and bind us all in health with one mind according to your will."*

Josem guided the men as he had his brothers through the murky Bog that seemed darker and even more dense than before. The stench was high as the storm had caused the mud to rise. The beasts moved slowly fighting to steady their hooves beneath them.

"Keep driving them forward!" Josem commanded when the beasts howled in protest. "We will be out of this soon!" Slowly they trudged through the densely wooded Bog and came to the end of the Outer Lands. They saw a bit of light break through the heavy clouds.

"I'll start down first. Every man follow behind me one by one. Mosimer you will be the last," Josem instructed.

"You need not spare an old man!" Mosimer shouted, forcing a smile from Josem. The first hill looked steep yet manageable, so Josem nudged his obstinate beast to start down. It planted its front hooves, then its second set, and then its third. When it tried to move its fourth set, its hind legs had slid the rest of the way down the slope and landed with a yelp on the grassy plateau below.

Josem patted the beast on its side to calm it and then reached into his tunic to retrieve what was left of a breaded treat. He whistled once to steady the creature. Predictably, it craned its neck as far back as it could to lick the soggy treat from Josem's hand with its long red tongue. "Very good boy, very good," he soothed, patting it again. Josem looked behind him to see his band of men. Though they were struggling they were successfully but clumsily navigating their beasts down the hill.

The next hill cut steeply into a narrow crevice before ending at another plateau. Josem clenched the reins in his cold wet hands as he spoke to the beast. "Take care, we must lead them to the Good King for Illiam's sake. Let's work together, aye?" A lightning bolt struck the ground to their right and the beast howled frantically stomping his hooves on the ground. Josem struggled to get the beast under control but it had startled again when the earth began to slide from under its feet. One of the men shouted, "Landslide!"

Mosimer cried out, "No, no, no, Josem!" as he watched in horror the land under Josem and his beast collapse. It happened so quickly that the men were frozen in shock. Mosimer dismounted and ran as close to the edge as he could. He could see that Josem's beast was dead and covered with earth. He tried to climb down but his men held him back.

"Josem!" he cried frantically, slipping into utter despair. "We cannot lose one!" he yelled. "*I've* done this! *I'VE DONE THIS!*" he repeated still searching the edge to see through the wind and the rain for Josem's body. He saw nothing. Pushing past his men he climbed down as carefully as he could to get a better look.

"Commander, it's not safe!" a Raider called out. "There's no way he could have survived a fall like that. He may be buried under his beast for all we know."

"Great One, have mercy on me!" Mosimer wept as his men drew him back up. He fell to his knees and grieved with his men beside him. His thoughts went instantly to the day when the King of the Hills People, Josem's father, had lost his life beneath his beast and how his own hope had been stripped in an instant.

The earth shook around them as the men hastened to their feet. A few of their beasts reared up on their hind legs as the men tried to move them to more secured ground.

"The earth is unsettled!" a Raider called out.

"Commander, we have to move!" cried another as he shivered in the rain.

Mosimer reluctantly stood as one of the Raiders helped him move as far away from the fallen earth as possible. The earth shook again.

"Look there!" one of the Raiders cried. "The winds are lifting the earth!"

"Something unnatural is happening!" cried out another. The earth flowed up as fast as it had slid away until it was as it had been before. The winds quieted, and the rain began to slacken. Mosimer ran to the edge to peer down. He gasped as he saw a frightened Josem climbing up the hill. He was completely covered in earth.

Mosimer cried out in pure joy, "My prince, give me your hand! My Lord, how much can my heart take?" Anxiously he reached down as far as he could. Josem grabbed his hand as soon as he was able and Mosimer pulled him up and into his arms. He hugged Josem hard, patted him on his back as tears coursed down his cheeks. "How my boy? How?" he asked in wonder. "No one but the Great One has spared you this very day."

Mosimer released Josem from his grasp. Josem stood before him, eyes wide with shock and brimming with tears. "What is it my son? Is there something else wrong?" Mosimer asked with concern. He heard the bellowing of the warring beast that had carried Josem before the fall. The men peered over the edge and saw the beast howling and shaking itself. A familiar figure held the reins. Mosimer pointed to the base of the cliff. "Josem look! The man you see down there is the King of the Plains People and a servant of the Great One. The man whom we effectually call a 'Good King'. Named from your own father's lips."

Josem began to shake as he moved away from the edge. Mosimer went to him and looked into his eyes.

"My life…the earth was removed from over me," Josem whispered, still in shock. "I couldn't breathe, hear, or see beneath the crushing rubble. I thought I was dead but I …awoke."

"I don't doubt it my dear boy. I don't doubt it! The Great One has great plans for you!" Mosimer said with a hearty laugh. His faith was instantly strengthened by the mercy of the Great One as enacted through his steward. "He's the first that I've known to command the earth. Now…Now do you see?"

Mosimer laughed so loudly that the sound echoed from the hills and cliffs around them. He looked into Josem's eyes and embraced him again. They waited on the cliff as the Good King rode the warring beast to them. Mosimer and his men greeted him with a bow and told him of their journey.

"I will follow you," said the Good King. Mosimer mounted his beast and instructed the men to prepare to head back toward the Southern Raider Camp in the Outer Lands.

*****

Early the next morning, Mosimer arrived first and with every man accounted for. Josem rode with Mosimer on his beast while the Good King followed at a distance. Josepher called for his son who was the same age Illiam had been when he made his vow as the band of men entered the camp.

"Where's your Good King? Did he refuse to come?" he asked mockingly as he grabbed the beast's reigns. He gave

Josem an appraising look as he dismounted. "Did you have a fall Josem? You've even lost one of your beasts in the futile effort I see. I can only imagine the disappointment." Josepher looked at Mosimer's men.

"It was all for the good," he declared directing his statement at Josem. "There is only one way to win this war that's coming just as I predicted. We must fight as one clan, one nation, under one king."

Josem stood still without saying a word. "Eason…" said Josepher, not fully noticing, "take the men to the stables so they may refresh their beasts." The boy obediently grabbed the reigns of Mosimer's beast, but the creature refused to move. The boy pulled the reigns as hard as he could, but the beast howled. Finally, it relented, almost causing Eason to fall. Other Raider clansmen hurried over to see what was happening. Josepher took the reins from his son in an effort to gain control of the beast himself. Mosimer and his men watched trying to conceal their amusement about the surprise Josepher was about to experience.

The beast eventually calmed and sat on the ground. The other beasts did the same. "Why are you all acting as if you have seen a ghost?" Josepher shouted in complete frustration as one by one, each man dismounted his beast, took a knee, and bowed. Josem being the last. "Why are you kneeling? Have you all lost your...?" Josepher's words tapered off as he noticed the figure in the distance riding what he assumed was Josem's beast covered in dried earth. "Is he...?" he said squinting his eyes. "It cannot be," he whispered.

As the brown figure drew nearer Josepher stood stunned and terrified. The Good King dismounted as the others began to stand.

"We are not insane, Josepher. We are just all of one mind toward the Great One," Mosimer said as the Good King approached Josepher with a smile. Though he only reached Josepher's chin, that didn't stop Josepher from feeling quite inadequate in comparison.

"Josepher, may I introduce you to the King of the Hills People?" Mosimer said feeling completely vindicated and overjoyed. Josepher stood back to get a better look at him. Attempting to overcome his initial shock, he cleared his throat.

"I expected you to be a larger man from the way they speak of you," he said.

The men talked and laughed as they dressed in the clean dry tunics given them. They ate and a few even napped as they waited for the beasts to be properly attended to. Everyone seemed at ease as though forgetting the urgency of the time. The Good King spoke only when spoken to, and when a soldier asked, he explained the peculiar reason he had found them when he did, and why he was in the land of the Hills People.

"Shortly after Illiam left I had a dream that I needed to follow him to the north. It wasn't clear to me why at the time but seeing your young prince fall brought more clarity to the purpose of my journey." he said.

"Josem is one of the youngest, but he has the tenacity of a predator." Mosimer added. "He insisted that we go even during the storm, and if we hadn't followed him, he would have gone to find you alone. Praise be to the Great One who made it well."

Experiencing what the Good King had done for him and watching his manner contradicted everything Josem had heard about him, except for what the Northern Raiders, Arlan, and his eldest brother Illiam had told him. He had become both amazed and anxious.

"Josepher, how much longer will it take for the beasts to be attended to? Our purpose for all that we're doing is still at hand," Josem blurted out in the middle of their conversation. The men stopped abruptly, surprised with the severity of his tone. The Good King said nothing.

"Well, once they've been fed and the dried mud cleaned off of their chains, saddles and hooves, they should be just as prepared and as eager as you are my prince," Josepher replied.

"Good!" Josem responded. He stood, stormed out of the tent, and began walking toward the stables to see the progress for himself when a voice stopped him in his tracks.

"Josem! You're back so soon!" It was Emil. A smile beamed from her excited face. She jumped into his arms and hugged him tightly before pushing herself away. "Never leave without telling me again," she said pointing her finger directly between his eyes. He drew her in and hugged her tightly. She fought to get loose but finally gave in when she noticed he wouldn't let go. She embraced him back until he released her enough for her to look into his eyes. "What's the matter?" she asked.

"You haven't heard? The Good King is here," he whispered in response. She gasped, eyes widening. "No wonder the camp has been in an uproar. Everyone has been whispering and running about in terror," she replied with a glance at Josepher's tent.

"That's not the worst part," he said.

"What is it, Josem?"

"I think I owe him my life...again."

As they walked to the stables, he told her everything that had happened during the storm the day before. She cried in his arms.

"You may hate me for saying this, Josem," she said attempting to wipe the tears that streamed down her cheeks that were flowing too quickly. "But you are nothing like your father. I've heard many stories about him Josem from the elder women here. If you were anything like him, I wouldn't have considered you, prince or not. Yet, he is still considered the hero of our people. He tormented and murdered anyone in his way. He was even willing to sacrifice *you* and your brothers out of selfish pride. You all were just small children for goodness' sakes! Yet and still, this man...this stranger among us...is the one we call a demon? Which one of them did the worst evil between them Josem? How would you judge?" She wept again, and he held her close.

Druds

A day later, Illiam had fully recovered from the effects of the small dose of Meraflax given to him. Unfortunately, according to his mother he still hadn't recovered enough. She demanded that he rest another day to be sure. She assigned one of her personal attendants to see to his needs and forbade him from doing anything for himself. The attendant came to him humbly and was very gentle and kind, even when she refused to sit and do nothing when he suggested it. He even went so far as to promise, on his honor, that he would keep it a secret. He noticed then that she was sweating heavily and thought she was falling ill.

"Are you well?" Illiam asked.

"Yes, my prince. It is just unusually warm for this time of year and I am a bit overdressed." Illiam searched her face.

"How long has it been this warm?" he asked.

"It happened suddenly my prince. Actually, it was just freezing a little while ago when I entered your tent," she replied. Illiam thanked her sincerely for her assistance and dismissed her for the day with no room for opposition. She left with little protest when she saw that he had begun to undress himself. He wanted to finally leave his bed and see for himself what was happening around him.

As he donned a fresh tunic, he heard a commotion near Arlan's tent.

*****

"I came to see the land of the mighty Raiders! All I've seen here are women and children, not men!" said a beastly man who was covered with hair and wore a thick beard and thick fur around his shoulders. He would easily have resembled and ancestor of the Raider Clan if not for his enormous height, rough beastly skin, extremely large arms, clawed hands, and jagged teeth.

"The Raiders that you seek have moved on," Arlan said. "We're farmers, traders and craftsman. We don't destroy, we create and cultivate the land."

"Great men were here and to the south before," he replied confused. "They must have found your people too weak to conquer. Even your Raiders thought you weren't worth the protection to stay and rule?" He looked at the members of the Raider Clan who had started to gather around. "If you're not warriors, you're slaves, but I am a god! I'm from a people who are warmed by the heat of the Catacombs within the mountains. We're always near the fire."

"Then why have you come here Drud?" Arlan asked boldly, using the folkloric name of the ancient nomadic people who were captured and deceived by the Wet Ones among the Catacombs. The brutish man looked him over and sniffed him.

"You don't smell or cower like a farmer…and you didn't run like a trader," he replied menacingly. "You're still an inferior meal of a man. But since you asked…I'll tell you. We're here to formally claim this territory for our queen Norishellke. The ruler of the Northern Territories among the Catacombs and Superior of all Kindlings…and 'Druds', as you call us. We will be bringing you all back as slaves. You'll work for us and have the privilege of keeping your lives for as long as we deem you necessary. Therefore, it would do you well not to waste anymore of my patience Hills People scum. I haven't had anyone to eat all day." He ground his teeth in frustration.

"How considerate of you to come alone and make such a charming proposition, but *we* decline it, demon. We are slaves to no one!" Arlan responded with equal disdain. The beastly man slapped Arlan across the face so hard that it knocked him to the ground.

"I have many members!" the beastly man shouted looking satisfied as people began to scream and scatter frantically. Nabe heard the commotion and ran past the women and children that were fleeing as far away from Arlan's tent as they could. He found his brother Arlan on the ground just as the brutish man reached forward to finish him off. Nabe let out a war cry. He reached beneath his tunic, withdrew a series of blades, and then skillfully hurled them at the man. The blades struck him in his shoulder, his neck, and the area between his right thumb, and pointed claw of his index finger. The blades immediately released poison into their target numbing him. More Raiders approached and surrounded the beastly man in their attack formations as the beastly man staggered back. The veins in his face began to protrude in shades of blue and purple. He laughed mockingly.

"Traders and farmers? Ha! Liars and cowards! Know that your judgement has come!" he shouted as he fell to his knees and gasped for air.

"What kind of being is this?" Illiam exclaimed as he strode to the brutish man and stood in front of him as Nabe helped Arlan to his feet. Illiam stood tall and confident as he watched the stranger grow weaker.

"Illiam, no!" Arlan cried out although he was still unsteady from the blow. Illiam wouldn't listen.

"And who might you be...boy?" the beastly man asked snarling as he struggled to speak.

"I used to know a man like you. He died as a cushion for a dead warring beast. His burial ground is right where the earth swallowed him up in a land that wasn't nor will ever be his. Your end will be quicker but not as merciful."

"Still...not as painful as yours, insolent boy," replied the brutish man. He reached for a knife sheathed on his right hip with his left hand. In a few swift motions he severed his right hand at the wrist and watched it fall to the ground. The brutish man laughed and then grimaced as his breathing became less fluid and the smell and taste of the poison entered his mouth. The amputated hand began to squirm and grow before their eyes. The Raiders stood repulsed not wanting to approach it.

"Take my brothers away from here and protect them with your life!" Arlan cried, turning to anyone who was near and capable. A few men hastened to Nabe to escort him away but Illiam wouldn't move. Nabe pulled away from the men and ran to stand beside Illiam as the beastly man fell to his side, still gasping while the hand continued to grow and take form. Arlan approached to pull them away himself when a group of shrieking flying beasts filled the sky darkening it. Nabe pointed up.

"Those are the beasts that followed us until we reached the bridge just before the strange wind. Josepher said that a demon was near when they arrived. If there were fewer then, what greater danger lies ahead of us now?" Nabe asked.

Just then, Illiam remembered the fear that had clenched his stomach when he had felt the unnaturally warm air and seen the flying beasts on their journey. He remembered how his hand had shaken on his blade as they had sought to defend themselves and how he'd been unable to focus. When he realized that he no longer felt the fear, he laughed at the brute in front of him.

Arlan however, was panicked. Breathing heavily, he struggled to drag his brothers away as they resisted. "Hurry! Take them from this place!" he commanded, trying to remove Illiam and Nabe from danger. No matter how much the Raider soldiers tried they couldn't move Illiam. He was way too heavy to carry away and so strong that he was able to shake them off with one swat of his hand and swing of his arm. The soldiers focused on Nabe instead.

"Arlan!" Nabe screamed. Not wanting to leave his brothers, he struggled as three Raider soldiers fought to drag him away from the dying brute and the abomination that continued to grow in front of their eyes. Torches were lit around the camp in order to see what was happening around them.

"Nabe you have to go!" Arlan demanded.

"I won't leave him Arlan!" Nabe cried briefly breaking his captors' hold. Nabe had never disobeyed a command before, and Arlan knew that he shared a bond with Illiam that couldn't be denied, but he didn't want to take any chances.

"Cease! Leave him alone!" commanded Illiam. The soldiers fearfully obeyed. Arlan turned to his older brother in anger.

"Are you still delirious? Do you think it is the Great One's will for you to die today?" he asked in frustration.

"Take heart, Arlan. Today you'll grow in faith," Illiam reassured him. "The Great One is still in control. Let him stay," he responded as he prayed inwardly for direction. Illiam didn't know why he had so much confidence. He understood Arlan's anxiety, but also knew that whatever evil this enemy had brought to the camp would come to an end, and at that moment, he wanted Nabe to see it.

"You fools! I am just a pawn...the least...of them!" gasped the beastly man. "Judgement has come!"

General Urius suddenly appeared. He was armed with his crossbow and the tips of the arrows in his hand were laced with Hilda's mixture. He moved between the brutish man and the princes and fired an arrow between the man's eyes. The hand continued to twist and curl as it created another form. This one was larger and fiercer than the last.

"I have even more members. I welcome you to free them all!" he cried. He then turned away from Illiam and charged toward a group of stunned Raiders who stood frozen with fear and killed them by biting, throwing and ripping them apart with his bare hands. The remaining Raiders began to attack him maniacally.

"What did that devil just unleash? I pray that Hilda's reputed poison still stands for that demon too." Urius said as he pursued him.

"General, do not dismember him, whatever you do!" Arlan shouted.

"Aye, kill that demon braggard but keep his body whole!" Urius commanded. He ran to assist the Raiders until the brutish form was overtaken.

A young Raider soldier holding a torch approached. "My prince, the bridge has been destroyed. The women, children, sick and elderly cannot escape!"

"How?" Arlan asked.

"We don't know my prince. What do you command?"

"Then they will stay and fight!" Illiam declared.

"Bring them back into the camp and arm them!" Arlan responded.

*****

Urius rejoined the princes in the center of the camp after the brutish man and his new form had been burned.

"These beasts that are circling are scavengers. Flesh eaters waiting as if our fate is sealed!" he shouted over the screeching sounds above them. Arlan gathered all the Northern Raider Clan that were able to fight and prepared them.

"There's a dark force here that has preyed on our minds and now wants our flesh," he said. "Today we will be victims to them no more. You Raiders have been chosen to protect the People of the Hills for many generations. Now, we risk every one of our lives to continue to defend our land, our people, and our faith. Where are our intercessors? Gather them," he instructed a Raider soldier.

"They're already assembled and have begun to pray," one of Urius's older sons replied. "Where they pray the beasts do not fly."

"How good of you to tell us this news NOW!" Urius screamed. "Nevertheless, lift your head, it is welcomed news," he added.

"Then we should all become intercessors, shouldn't we?" Nabe asked.

"Speak quickly, brother," Arlan commanded.

"Have Raiders positioned along the perimeter of our borders in groups of ten. Put ten soldiers on the front line and have about seven intercessors behind them. Have no less than twenty intercessors placed at the threshold of our camp where the demon entered in the north and the same number where the bridge was destroyed to the south. Seven intercessors and ten soldiers to keep watch at the east and western perimeters. Let them all be of the same mind. Tell them to pray in the places assigned to them to restrict the flying beasts from entering the sky above the camp. Whatever threat is looming communicates with these beasts. We need to send a message as well. The rest will remain here to do the same. It may be possible that when the enemy sees this, they will become confused. They may flee or at least afford us more time to seek the Great One for guidance."

Nabe turned to Arlan. "What do you say, brother?" Arlan nodded quickly and patted Nabe on the back in gratitude.

"You've heard your young prince!" Arlan called out to the surrounding crowd. "Urius take your sons and start dividing our clansmen as he has said. Then meet me in the north where the brute entered our camp. You and I will join the ten to keep watch over the intercessors there. Nabe and Illiam will remain here in the center."

"I would prefer to be at the bridge," Nabe requested earnestly. Arlan looked at his brave and wise younger brother and grabbed him by the scruff of the neck. He drew his forehead to his own and said, "The fact that I don't dig a hole where you stand and stuff you both into it to save your lives should be enough Nabe. Since you're stuck here to fight for your life, I'm comfortable with you being the last of us to do so. Now, where is Illiam?" Arlan asked, looking out and noticing that his brother was gone. "Also, bring my mother here. We'll need a seer to alert us to what the Great One is saying. I'll need the two of you to watch over Illiam until he's strong again."

"He didn't seem weak at all. You have forgotten that you and your men tried to carry him away without success," Nabe said.

"I saw him near your tent a while ago my prince, where the demon appeared," a nearby Raider responded.

*****

Raiders were groomed for war all their lives but the unspoken terror of what lay ahead hung heavy in the air.

"Hurry to your assigned stations!" Urius yelled out. "This place has the stench of fear flowing through it!" He slammed his large foot against a wooden crate filled with vegetables causing it to crack open violently and spill its contents onto the ground. "That smell is like sweet nectar to these blood thirsty beasts! Pray and arm yourselves!" Urius ranted. "There will be no more Raider blood dampening these grounds!"

He ordered everyone to their posts as the people clamored, ran and scattered around to equip themselves and move to their assigned posts. Groups of children began to pray as a few elders found their weapons of choice.

"Elders prepare to remind us what real war looked like in your time because your hour has come again! Those who are ill, fight for your lives as if no one else will. Defend what you believe in with joy, and the knowledge that your last breath may save another!" Urius then looked to the women. "You women!" he called out glancing at his wife as she stood with his youngest children. "Many of you wield swords better than your fathers, brothers, sons…and husbands. Bravely use your legendary skills with elixirs as you fight, heal and protect." The women scattered and gathered their concoctions and small children. Many distributed weapons among themselves and the soldiers as they ran past on foot or thundered by on their beasts.

"If you or your children can't carry swords, use rocks! Fight, and never give yourselves over to fear!" Urius instructed. He made one last round before he moved to the northern threshold of the Raider Camp. He ignited the people to defend themselves against the terror they had created for others in generations past.

The First Earth Warrior

osimer and his men mounted their beasts and prepared to leave the Southern Raider Camp. Josem mounted his own faithful beast while the Good King sat astride Josepher's favorite for the journey to the Northern Outer Lands. The two horns on the sides of its head curled toward one another and crested like a crown on top. Its neck was covered with gold bands, its clawed hooves were painted in gold and gold chains swung from its hooves and saddle. When the chains rattled, they produced a chiming sound that Mosimer argued was 'inappropriate for battle'.

Josepher swallowed hard and replied, "It's fit for a king, and since you call him a good one, it can't hurt much now, can it?" With a nod of gratitude and a smile of amusement the

Good King rode forward with Mosimer, Josem and their men close behind him. Josepher and the Southern Raider Clan were relieved that the Good King hadn't destroyed them as he had been fabled to do as they watched them ride away.

*****

Back in the Northern Raider Camp everyone had either dispersed to their assigned places or was sitting in prayer in the center of camp. The flying beasts hovered in the sky but had moved from directly overhead. As Illiam emerged from Arlans tent, a small blade in his hand, Nabe approached and told him what everyone in the camp was assigned to do. He was told how the intercession was restricting the enemy's ability to fly beyond the camp perimeter allowing more daylight to enter in.

"How long will they do this?" Illiam asked. "If the scavengers are still flying above, they are clearly expecting something. Something more than scouts and Druds is coming...I just know it. Where is Arlan now?"

"He and General Urius and other soldiers are guarding the intercessors at the northern perimeter, where they believe the brute entered. He requested that we stay here where it is safe," Nabe replied.

"Tell me, brother, do you feel safe?" Illiam pressed.

He shook his head. "Not at all. You've heard that the bridge has been destroyed and that Mosimer and his men haven't returned," Nabe replied. "Remember Arlan sent them to find the Good King while you were asleep."

"And my mother? Have you seen her anywhere?"

"For now, she is safe here in the camp. She is a seer Illiam. She said that she saw death and destruction, but she told us not to fear. She said we will have victory because the Great One will be sending help."

*****

Josepher returned to his tent and recalled how he had watched the Good King, Mosimer, Josem, and their band of Raiders start their journey to the north to revive their sleeping prince. It seemed more like a fairytale than anything else. He remembered his conversation with this King of the Plains People and laughed in disbelief.

"You're not as tall or as fierce as I thought…" he said, his words echoing in the large empty space. "But there's something about you that caused our esteemed Commander

Mosimer, General Urius, and our princes to trust you with their lives." He reached for his skin of mixed wine, a concoction made only by the artisans among his tribesmen in the north but found it empty. He sighed and sat on his raised cushioned bed. Deep in thought, he combed his fingers through his beard.

"What if, for just one moment, he is who they have said?" He looked at the cushion where the Good King had sat earlier. "What is this Great One anyway? Will he unite our tribe? Will we be established? Will our princes fulfill their destinies? What if indeed." He stretched out on his bed and fell into a deep sleep.

He startled awake when a horn blew just a half hour later.

"Father!" Eason shouted in fear as he burst into the tent. "What is it, boy?" he asked sitting abruptly.

"Didn't you hear the horns? The watchmen have reported that the northern camp is on fire! They've seen smoke rise like an eruption," Eason blurted out. Two men followed him into the tent. They saluted and confirmed what Eason had said.

"Commander, the men are ready for your instructions!" the first said standing at attention as he awaited a response.

Josepher looked around bewildered and then straitened himself enough to finally say, "Then prepare for battle. We are finally at war!"

Raider soldiers quickly mounted their warring beasts. Boys were considered men the moment they learned to ride the massive creatures. They became Raiders when they learned how to fight with them. Everyone with the ability to ride followed Josepher to the north to defend or avenge their clansmen. Though uncertain of the outcome Josepher was determined. Meeting the Good King so many hours before and then setting out to fight what he knew would be a battle against the very extinction of his people was all a blur to him. In a daze, he had bid farewell to his child and clansmen, then set out with his fierce army to fight the unknown.

Two hundred fought as though they were two thousand once the Raiders mounted their beasts. Therefore, the strength of their 20,000 soldiers shook the earth. The sight and sound of the Raiders was menacing as they overwhelmed the Outer Lands with their numbers. Josepher longed for mixed wine more than ever to numb the nauseating thought that all his people, his princes, Isha Hilda, Mosimer and even his older most stubborn brother, Urius, might require a burial ceremony. Especially Urius. "That dumb braggard," he growled pushing his beast to move faster over the hills and urging his men to match his quickened pace. As he saw smoke rise to obscure the mountains beyond, he blew his horn. If any of his clansmen in the north were still alive, they'd know that help was on the way.

*****

The Good King, Josem, Mosimer, and the band of Raider soldiers hastened through the forest and summited the high hills on their beasts. The creatures seemed nimbler and the earth seemed to tremble as they trampled it beneath their hooves. As they reached the southern perimeter of the camp, they slowed in wake of devastation. The bridge was gone and there were flying scavenger beasts circling the cliff. Men lay dead, while a few survivors tried in vain to fight off the scavengers. Smoke rose in the distance from the direction of the Northern Raider camp. The Good King dismounted as the men watched in horror." Great One, what has happened?" Mosimer cried out.

The Good King walked to the edge of the cliff and stepped off. The earth groaned and shifted beneath him springing up to form a new bridge to the other side of the valley. It happened so quickly that Mosimer was tempted to stop just to watch in awe. The Good King's creature followed him. Josem, who had already dismounted, ran behind him, and was followed by his own beast and the rest of the men. When the Good King reached the other side, the scavengers recoiled in fear and fled the injured along the path.

"These men who lie here are our soldiers and intercessors," Mosimer explained aggrieved as he joined the Good King. One of the men who had survived cried out, "Commander, please help! Some of the soldiers were overcome by the Dark Voice!"

"One of them even began rambling," cried another. "He was saying things that we couldn't understand, like 'One of many!' and 'She is waiting!' before he attacked. They've headed toward the camp."

"Carry them," the Good King said to the beasts. Instantly, the three that carried the Good King, Mosimer and Josem lowered themselves to their knees and allowed the soldiers to load as many of the dead and injured onto their backs as they could carry. As the men moved forward, they heard the screams and cries of the people as they ran through the smoke and fire that had ravaged the camp.

Men, women, and children lay dead. Lifeless creatures were strewn among them. Mosimer grabbed a Raider soldier who was running and bleeding from his head.

"What's happening?"

"They've come! All of them! Druds…from the mountains…the Catacombs! How can we defeat our own men? How can we survive against rock and fire?" the soldier replied deliriously. They heard a thud as a large rock hit the earth. A moan came from above and then another loud thud. All around them tents full of supplies were flattened and engulfed in the flames. A screaming group of women struggled to pull a limp young girl away.

"Send word to Josepher that we're under attack," Mosimer instructed his two best riders. "If his watchmen have eyes in their skulls, they should see that our camp is in flames?" The riders galloped away on their beasts, horns at the ready to alert their southern clansmen. "Don't let anything hinder you!" Mosimer shouted as they approached the earthen bridge.

"You five…" the Good King said, pointing at the Raiders, "Lead everyone you can find away from the camp and across the bridge to safety. If I see any other Raiders, I will send them to help you." The men covered their faces as their beasts bellowed and reared up on their two sets of hind legs. They hurried to direct all the people they could find away from the smoke and flames.

Just then, a whooshing sound came from over-head. A flaming boulder rocketed from out of the smoke and hurled toward the bridge. It crashed in front of the Raiders and survivors who were attempting to cross, but the bridge expanded both its width and its depth to catch the boulder and extinguish the flames. The people gazed in astonishment. Some more terrified by the bridge than by the horror they were fleeing. Some had to be dragged and carried to the other side, but many rejoiced saying "The Great One is with us! Look, even the bridge defends us!" The Good King disappeared into the smoke. Josem followed him.

"Josem!" Mosimer cried out.

"I have to find my brothers!" Josem replied, the same determined look in his eyes that had led him to venture into the deadly storm.

"Don't die," Mosimer pleaded, the warmth of a father in his voice. He had assumed the role the day the King of the Hills People had perished.

"That's entirely up to the Great One, isn't it?" Josem replied with a smirk as he covered his face with his hood and ran farther into the camp.

"The two of you, follow him," Mosimer instructed the Raiders at his right. Eagerly, the men followed Josem into the smoke and chaos on their beasts.

*****

A small group of Raider soldiers appeared on foot. The highest ranking among them hurried in shock to Mosimer.

"Commander, there are Druds advancing. They're beastly men. They emerged after you were commissioned. The first of them struck Arlan and was taken down by Nabe and Urius, but before he died, he multiplied himself into another worse than himself."

"What do you mean 'multiplied himself'?" Mosimer asked.

"If he is dismembered in the slightest way, he reproduces himself from that, sir."

"What an abomination! What kind of beings are these?" Mosimer asked in disgust. "Then prepare to run them through without shredding them! Pile them up with poisons and burn them with the fire they've created!" he shouted as the men cheered. "Return to the foot of the bridge. Do not worry for it has been divinely re-created!" Mosimer roared. One Raider dismounted his beast and gave him to Mosimer to ride. "Wait for the remnant of the camp to arrive and treat and prepare those who need immediate care." The Raiders on foot saluted and moved to the bridge. "The rest of you will come with me. Let us do our part and introduce our enemies to *our* way of battle. May the Great One keep our souls and be ever with us!

"Lord be with us!" the men cried in unison. Mosimer lifted his horn and blew it so loudly that the Raiders who were lost in confusion looked up and were heartened that he had returned.

"Leave none of them alive!" he shouted as they charged bravely into the dense smoke and flames, faces covered, and beasts armed. Dozens upon dozens of the Druds were hidden among the flames. Each was taken down as the Raiders stealthily trapped and poisoned them. Some trampled them with their warring beasts. Piles of them were set on fire in mounds that resembled boulders when seen through the thick smoke. Although the fiery boulders had changed the landscape of their camp, the Raiders were able to adjust their tactics and stayed true to their objective.

*****

The area to the east of the Northern Raider camp was completely devastated. Fiery boulders had crushed and scorched every structure built after the initial attack from the northern perimeter. Although Arlan, Urius and a few others had managed to escape the northern perimeter, they were scattered and found themselves running from innumerable Drud soldiers. Arlan helped the intercessors escape as Urius and a few other soldiers led the Druds away to the east near the Sharp Cliffs.

"What's that I hear? Is it Mosimer's horn?" General Urius whispered. He was lying trapped beneath pieces of fallen rock, ash and debris from the tents and stone keeps that had been crushed by the boulders. He had just killed two Drud beings and, unfortunately, one of his own clansmen who had attacked him from behind when he thought Urius was unaware. In shock, but rich in instinct, Urius had turned and caught him in the neck with the last of the blades hidden under his sleeve. The soldier had grabbed him gasping and gurgling his regrets.

"Great One, my Lord, what kind of evil could take the minds of our men?" he prayed, bleeding heavily from the wound in his side. "If, by some miracle, you allow me to live, because I am quite vulnerable now, teach me how to battle without physical weapons. If I had known, my clansman's blood wouldn't be on my hands." He fought back tears and struggled to remain conscious as he tried to distract himself from the pain and increasing weakness by closing his eyes and humming a faint tune.

A few moments later Urius heard a grunting sound. Bracing himself, he heard a voice say, "I traveled here to help an ill brother and now this? What has happened, General?" Josem approached Urius with two Raider soldiers behind him on their large warring beasts. Urius laughed until he coughed painfully.

"My prince!" he gasped. "It has been a while, but I should know a brother of Arlan by now when I see one. Which one are you?"

"I am Josem." As gently as they could, Josem and his men removed Urius from the debris that had trapped and wounded him. Urius told them where to find Arlan's tent and rode with the Raider who was strong enough to support his weight behind him. The tent was no longer standing.

"I'm sorry my prince. If by some miracle they are alive, then they're either hiding among the debris or have somehow escaped toward the western perimeter if it hasn't been overtaken already." Random shouting and screams sounded from all around them, but they could hardly see through the fire and smoke that became thicker and more toxic by the minute.

"Do not worry," Josem said. "I will take you to the bridge so you can be cared for, and then I'll return to look for them. That is the way we came through with the Good King." He motioned toward the south. Urius' eyes widened in surprise. "Yes!" Josem replied as he looked into the eyes of an obviously weakened man. "He was sent by the Great One before we could even request it."

"Then it will be well!" Urius proclaimed. Another crash behind them sent their beasts running trampling Druds as they passed through the smoke and what remained of the Northern

Raider Camp. Other Raider soldiers fought bravely as they made their way toward the bridge alongside them.

When Josem arrived at the bridge with General Urius, more than a dozen Raider soldiers were present with their beasts, ready to lead their clansmen out of the chaos and to safety on the other side. The Raider who carried the general lowered his beast so that Urius could be removed and have his wound tended to. Josem dismounted and rushed over to help. Urius grabbed Josem's arm and pulled him closer with his remaining strength and whispered, "You and your men take care. Our enemies wear our faces, and they aren't aware that they've turned until it's too late."

"I know," Josem replied, noting that Urius had turned pale. "A few of them who were here with the intercessors attacked and killed many before they returned to the camp, but you must rest. It *will* be well." He turned to a soldier. "Here, take him across the bridge," he instructed. "He has lost a lot of blood from the wound on his side."

Looking around, he saw Raiders leading people hurriedly across the bridge. "Has anyone seen any of my brothers?"

"No, my prince, but recently we escorted Isha Hilda away. She is now on the other side. She and only a few others are tending to the wounded," one replied. Closing his eyes in relief, Josem mounted his beast and rode back into the battle leaving Urius in the Raiders' care.

*****

Just an hour before Urius was found, Illiam and Nabe felt a huge startling thud that shook the ground. Screams emanated from all around them.

"Fire!" people cried. They tried to extinguish the gigantic flaming boulders that had flown over their heads, crashed, and killed or trapped many of their clansmen. Raiders worked to rescue anyone who was alive until a second thud came, followed by a third that sent the camp into utter chaos.

"What direction are they coming from?" Nabe demanded as they hurriedly searched for a path away from the center of the camp.

"From the north! All of the rocks are being hurled from the north!" Illiam shouted as they dodged the smoke and flames.

"Illiam…, Arlan was at the perimeter in the north with the intercessors! It must have been breached!" Nabe cried.

"Maybe, if our enemies are hurling fiery rocks, it may be because they could not enter that easily. They are making a way for something else to enter, but do not lose hope!" Illiam exclaimed as the two ran and dodged the falling debris. A sound rang out. "What is that?" Illiam asked.

"It's a horn. It is the call of Commander Mosimer. He has returned!" Nabe cried, encouraged. "We should try to move toward it."

On the ground, a soldier whose legs were trapped cried out. Close by, another lay dead, his body engulfed in flames.

"Help me!" the trapped soldier cried out again. Nabe patted out the flames as Illiam moved the heavy fragments on him, lifted the soldier effortlessly, and slung him over his shoulder. Seeking refuge as far away as possible, the two found themselves weaving through the new landscape toward the western perimeter.

Nabe was amazed by Illiam's strength. His steps were swifter than Nabe's, even while carrying the soldier. Nabe decided to reserve his questioning and hurried to help the children who were crying and separated from their parents along the way. He carried a young child and encouraged the older ones to follow. Many soldiers grabbed the injured and weak while others wrangled the warring beasts that had been startled and scattered. Others tried to douse the fire with barrels of water, but it was spreading too quickly.

"Did you hear the horn of Mosimer?" Nabe asked a Raider soldier who was riding past with his wife and children on one beast and two more harnessed closely behind. "It was toward the southern perimeter. Take them in the direction of the sound you heard. Hurry!" The Raider quickly dismounted his beast and left the reigns in his wife's hands. He mounted one of the other beasts as Nabe and Illiam draped the injured across it. The children were placed on the last beast with the eldest at the rear. She held the reigns as best she could as they hastened toward Mosimer's horn.

Two more Raiders arrived on their beasts and began to assist.

"There isn't much refuge at the perimeter in the east. The brutes are not alone," said one.

"We'll carry who we can too but have the others who can run follow us to the south," said the other. "I was told the bridge has been restored and to lead whoever is left out of the camp by the Goo…" He continued until he realized who he was addressing. "Our princes!" he said in surprise. Saluting awkwardly, he moved to climb down from his saddle to allow them to ride.

"No! Do not dismount." said Illiam. "Take my brother, but I will stay and help."

"I will not leave you, Illiam!" Nabe said determinedly.

"This all began shortly after I arrived. Since the Dark Voice has tormented *me* about this day, I will see it to the end," Illiam said determinedly.

"Then so will I!" Nabe proclaimed. "Do what you were charged to do, and I will lead whoever I can deeper within the camp toward you. It is getting too dangerous for you to go any deeper into the camp than here. We still haven't found Isha Hilda and Arlan. Alert the others," he commanded the Raiders. Looking toward the direction of the bridge he saw a few younger soldiers stopping to catch their breath. Nabe went over to one of them and took his pouch filled with water around his waist to drink from it. Then he ran back dodging flames and broken smoldering rocks and debris with Illiam close behind.

Nabe covered his mouth but the thickening smoke was beginning to fill his lungs. He began coughing uncontrollably until he fell to his knees. In one swift movement, Illiam grabbed him by the arm and helped him to his feet. He wrapped Nabe's arm around his neck and they ran through the heat, smoke, and flames at an extraordinary speed. Illiam could hear the cries, screams, groans, and moans of the victims and wished that he could see through the smoke. Another whoosh sounded overhead followed by a crash. It seemed to be closing in as more of the boulders landed. One Raider, arms full of possessions looked for a path through the clouds of darkness. "Leave your goods behind and look for your clansmen who need you! They are what cannot be replaced!" Illiam shouted angrily. The man was startled, peered at him, and then disappeared behind a cloud of smoke.

Illiam felt a hand against his chest as Nabe wordlessly sought his attention.

Great One, help us! Illiam prayed. He lay Nabe on the ground where the air was somewhat clearer and watched him breathe in gasps. Illiam tried to look around for others. He saw Raiders that had been left behind trapped and scattered in the darkness, choking and gagging from the smoke. Somehow, he could see them clearly. "Great One, I don't know how this is possible but please help me lead them out of this hell!"

Crouching protectively over his brother, he drew a breath and looked toward the others.

"To the southern perimeter!" Illiam shouted into the smoke. "Where you hear my voice, run!" He continued to yell, unaffected by the atmosphere around him. The others began to blindly run toward him. He covered Nabe who struggled to breathe, as some bumped into and stumbled over them. Clansmen and women covered in soot with burned skin and charred clothing ran past him. "Keep running and don't look back, no matter what you see or hear!" he shouted. "Go toward the bridge. Do not fear but trust the Great One alone!"

Some fell and were overcome by the flames and choking air. Illiam looked down at Nabe who coughed less frequently. He lifted him to his feet again but Nabe could hardly stand.

"I'll carry you to the bridge if I have to, brother," he said hoisting him onto his shoulder.

As Illiam turned to follow the crowd, something slammed into his face. He fell to one knee and an unconscious Nabe landed on the ground a few feet away in the darkness. Illiam struggled to regain his senses. As he turned to see what struck him, he was knocked onto his back.

"We told you that we were many! We are always near the fire," a brutish voice scoffed as a kick to Illiam's side sent a sharp pain across his chest. The brute leaned over him. "To the south, you say?" Others, each more brutish than the next emerged from the smoke to stand behind him. "Who could have been foolish enough to restore what we have broken?" the creature mocked. "Know that there is no one greater than those who devour you today."

Illiam tried to move but the pain made it impossible. Even breathing was unbearable. He closed his eyes and anger rose up inside him. When he opened them again, he could see more brutish men approaching him through the darkness as others fled toward the bridge. His eyes watered from the pain. He closed them and waited for them to finish him off, but the moment never came. He looked through the smoke but saw no one. He felt himself losing consciousness.

A few moments later, he heard a familiar voice whisper, "Illiam." He peered from side to side, but no one was there. He closed his eyes and opened them again to see a man standing right in front of him. As the man walked closer the smoke around him began to clear. He saw that it was the King of the Hills People and the prophet of the Great One. Illiam's eyes widened with surprise as he tried to control his breathing and the pain it caused.

"Good King…you're here?" he whispered faintly.

"What has happened, boy?" the Good King asked. He knelt beside Illiam as the smoke continued to dissipate. Illiam glimpsed at the ruined camp around them.

"My brother…Nabe…I can't find him," Illiam gasped.

"He is strong, Illiam. He will be well." The Good King broke the earth beside him with his fist and watched it crumble. After a quick prayer, he gathered a handful and sifted it back and forth between his fingers, over and over until the moisture from his hands turned it into a thick paste. Illiam whimpered and groaned in agony as he was rolled onto his side. The Good King rubbed the earth over the area where his ribs had been shattered. The earth changed form, molding around Illiam and instantly hardening. Then the Good King gently readjusted the ribs that had been broken.

"You have been transformed. I can see that it has already begun, or you would be dead by now," said the Good King. He stood as the earth continued its work. Illiam's groans subsided, and his breathing became less strained. The Good King walked over to Nabe, who was still unconscious on the ground.

A Change of Heart

The two Raiders who were sent by Commander Mosimer to alert Josepher and the Southern Raiders were shocked when they felt the rumbling of the earth and saw the border between the Southern and Northern Outer Lands breached by a massive army of warring beasts and men charging toward them. They heard the horn of Josepher and glanced at each other in relief. They waited until they could see the eyes of their clansmen before they turned and raced back to the camp, leading them to the devastation ahead.

As his beast sped ahead of the massive army, Josepher blew his horn in hopes that it would strike fear in any enemy who would dare harm his people. He slowed his stride, however, when he reached large scattered groups of what remained of the men, women, children, beasts, and livestock that had been rescued from the northern camp. Some of the Raiders cheered as they saw the riders pass. Others shouted, "Hurry, hurry!" and pointed toward the northern camp desperately wanting their southern brethren to help their clansmen escape the evil that seemed intent on destroying them.

"Continue to move as many of our clansmen that are able to the southern camp!" Josepher ordered to a few of his Raiders. "Bring our healers to retrieve the rest who are not. Has anyone seen our princes?"

"Not here Commander Josepher, but our Prince Josem has been going deep into the fire and leading our clansmen to the bridge to escape. He brought your brother, Urius, who was injured and near the entrance of the bridge being prepared to be carried over," one soldier answered from among the survivors.

Josepher's stomach dropped. *Being prepared?* He thought. "Son…" With hesitation he asked, "Is he…?"

"No Commander, he was still alive…but…he is injured badly," the young man responded before Josepher could finish asking his question. Josepher spurred his beast to a gallop and rode, followed by his men, to the edge of the cliff where the bridge had been. He remembered how the unnatural wind had pushed him back when he had arrived at the bridge the last time, and he was determined not to let it hinder him again. To his surprise he found a structure unlike anything he had ever seen before.

The bridge stood high. It was fortified with earth and the vines twined under and along the length of it soaring into the air. It was both a frightening and magnificent creation that would have taken decades to complete, even by the hands of hundreds of master craftsmen. His eyes widened and his heart raced as he and his men approached. Josepher's first thought as he crossed that magnificent bridge was his last conversation with Urius when he had questioned his faith and his sanity. His brothers' decided response echoed in his mind.

"A man who has learned that who is for him is greater than who's against him. There will come a time when you'll have to choose a side. If that miserable threat shows itself at your door, then what real power will be on your side, Josepher?"

Inexplicable hope grew inside Josepher. His brother's words and the unique structure that he now traversed both pointed to the possibility that there may actually be a "Great One."

Josepher halted his beast when he came upon the soldiers who had secured Urius with straps of cloth and leather. When the men saw him, they stepped aside. Josepher drew near and called to his brother.

"Urius, are you well?" At first Urius did not respond, but suddenly he squinted and coughed, "Better than you, you braggard," he rasped. Josepher dismounted his beast and commanded his generals to follow the scouts sent before them. "Also, find Josem and do as he says," he ordered. On the soldier's command, the beast that carried Urius lowered itself as Josepher dismounted.

"So, you're alive," he said, grabbing his brother's hand.

"Alive in spirit, brother, but weak in body," Urius muttered. Josepher looked him over and saw the bloodied bandages wrapped around his middle.

"Has anyone given him anything to treat this?" he asked, anxiously reaching for the vial of Meraflax that he carried around his neck.

"Commander, he has refused it," replied one of the soldiers. "He told us not to waste it."

Josepher looked at Urius in desperation. "Pull through until I return, brother. You have children and a people who still need you." He squeezed Urius' hand. Urius returned the gesture weakly and said in a faint voice, "Josepher…Your hope will be fulfilled. You will live to see our people…united…under one king and one God, but…I will have to see it from above." Then he closed his eyes for the last time.

Josepher kissed his brother's forehead. "You've fought well."

The Dark Queen

Toward the northern perimeter stood the Dark Queen, Norishellke. She had the face of a reptile and a tail that swung and rattled when she walked. Her tall body swayed as she looked to and fro observing the destruction around her. She asked her general in frustration, "Where are the Raiders?"

"They're running away. Many of them have already escaped."

"Are you sure these are the Raider Clan? I've waited too long for this." The Drud General nodded swiftly. "I have called for the rest among them. What is the delay?" she asked. "Go and summon the rest of your brothers and sisters. If the Raiders that I turned fail in infiltrating and deceiving them, we'll have to move quickly." The general left with a horde of Druds following him.

Senses heightened; the Dark Queen sniffed the air. "Something is wrong. We should have gotten them all by now."

"Are you referring to me?" Arlan asked limping out from behind a massive boulder and brandishing a sword coated with blood, "It seems that I have escaped your ambush as well." He moved closer to the Dark Queen leaving himself completely vulnerable.

"Hmm, Raider Clan! I could smell you in the distance. Have you come to surrender?"

"Surrender to what? And for what reason?" he asked brazenly.

"Don't you understand what you have done? All of you are guilty!" said the Dark Voice. Startled, Arlan glanced around him.

"As far as I know we are not guilty of anything! What right do you have to judge us?" he asked, looking at her again.

"Aren't you an heir? You are one of the sons of the king of these lands, aren't you? He owes us a debt and has not repaid for all that he has acquired. He promised us ten sons, but you have been kept from us," the Dark Queen responded. "And now here you are."

"My father brought the judgement of his sins upon his own head!" Arlan retorted. He didn't notice that she was suddenly closer to him until her tail rattled.

"But you're not the eldest, are you?" she asked, looking at him suspiciously. "Where is he? He's been called."

"All of you are mine!" the Dark Voice shrieked, causing Arlan to wince.

"And I'm here to collect you!" she added, enraged. She peered around as though sensing something but then returned her focus to Arlan.

The Good King is not the first my father sacrificed us to, Arlan thought. *If he couldn't sell his children, he'd obligate us to avenge him with blind loyalty to him as our father and king.* Anger began to rise inside of him toward his father's betrayal. He began to understand the torment that Illiam had experienced. It was hard to focus on the Dark Queen as he struggled to think.

The Dark Queen moved closer again. In a blink, she was just four yards away. Suddenly Mosimer's face entered his mind. Arlan thought of the man who replaced the king and father who had failed him. He was blessed to know the love of a *real* father and his thoughts became clear.

"My brothers and my clan belong to the Great One," Arlan told her as he tightened his grip on his weapon. He glared intently at her monstrous face and thought she might have been a woman once behind her bright scales and reptilian eyes. Now she resembled a malformed hybrid of a woman and beast. "Are you their queen?" he asked.

"I'm their queen and mother!" she cooed with pride.

"Is your ultimate goal to enslave us?" he asked plainly in an effort to distract her.

"Those we don't devour…Yes!" she hissed, her brow furrowing as she began to grind her jagged teeth.

"Then we are at an impasse," Arlan concluded. "I have no intention of surrendering."

She hissed again. "*You cannot win!*" the Dark Voice screamed. Arlan winced once more at its cutting sound.

Great One, it's so loud! Arlan prayed. *This is how they fight. They destroy from within.*

"If you are the mother of these Drud brutes, then what created you?" he asked in defiance evoking her fury.

"So, you mock me! I'm sure you will be missed. It's a shame that I will have to crush your bones into the earth," she said, looking around again as though hearing something. "Even if, by some impossibility, you defeat me, my children are here now, and you are alone."

Arlan's stomach dropped and his heart began to beat rapidly as he heard the sound of brutes marching toward him. One by one, they began to appear through the fire and thick smoke. *It has finally come to this*, he thought, the nausea that he usually felt in battle coming to the fore. *This is how I die.* Although, Arlan had always wondered more about *when* he would die rather than how. He didn't expect to grow as old as Urius or Mosimer, but he had hoped that it would be long before his younger brothers. He had always known that he ran the risk that they would feel the loss he felt with Illiam. Above all else, he had hoped that if he were to die in battle, he would be fighting for the glory of the Great One.

Arlan took a deep breath and braced himself to deal as many deadly blows as he could before he took his last breath.

"He is never alone," said the Good King casually, standing behind Arlan. Arlan looked around in shock. The Dark Queen screamed and fell to the ground, hissing and writhing about at the sight of him. She scuttled away from him, waving away things around her that couldn't be seen.

"No!" she screamed. "They belong to us! Why are you here?" she groaned as all her Drud children thrashed about in pain and fear blinded where they stood.

"You should know who stands with him. The princes will bring misery to your descendants for all time. You have come to claim their lives today because of their father's sin, but your influence over him has been evident. You have bewitched their father in order to claim his sons. You have done this for many generations. The Great One has seen and has brought me here to claim *your* flesh this day."

Norishellke began to beg as the earth swallowed her children alive, silencing their torment until she was completely alone.

"You have said that you're always near the fire…let's return you to it," the Good King said. He lifted his right leg and stomped hard on the ground, causing the earth around the Dark Queen to crumble. A hot and fiery abyss opened and grew between them. Arlan saw that the fire was blue with white smoke that wafted high into the air. He wanted to run from what he was seeing but couldn't move.

Struggling to stand, the Dark Queen summoned her flying beasts to rescue her with a screech that resembled theirs, but as they came near, the abyss drew them into the fire. Unable to resist her call, they came one by one. Each was drawn into the fire and was no more. The Dark Queen darted her eyes at Arlan with a hatred and rage like he had never seen before. In that moment, he felt complete fear. She was so menacing that he was about to look away, but the rising smoke obscured her sight. It began to burn her eyes and singe her flesh. As she screamed and writhed in pain the earth narrowed under her feet. She lost her balance and followed her offspring into the deep chasm of fire.

Trembling, Arlan fell to his knees. He had heard stories about this king and what he could do with the authority bestowed upon him by the Great One. He had even seen in

his camp the power of the miraculous through intercession…
but never this. Never had he faced an adversary this fierce that
had been overcome… and without weapons.

The earth remained open. When the Good King saw
Arlan's bewilderment, he said, "More will enter. Come, there
is more to do. No one knows that you are still alive." Arlan
arose and turned to follow him.

*****

The camp was filled with the stench of burnt wood and
flesh, though most of the fire had been doused by the heavy
snow that was beginning to cover the ruins in a thick blanket
of white. Arlan and the Good King began their journey toward
the south to rejoin the remainder of the Raider Clan. The huge
boulders had created a labyrinth, but as they approached each
mountainous wall, it shifted out of their way. Arlan had many
questions for the Good King, but he remained silent as he
followed and observed the new landscape around him of what
was left of his home.

The snow piled up quickly shrouding the remains of those
who had perished, be they friend or enemy.

"They will all be gone when you return. Do not worry." said the Good King. "Every foe who lay among your people today will cease to exist." Arlan marveled as each Drud soldier dissolved before their eyes under the mounds of snow. All was quiet. It even seemed peaceful as Arlan continued to limp behind the Good King. His heart swelled with awe, grief, and gratitude.

Arlan swooned as they walked across the earthen bridge that had replaced the one that had been destroyed. As they moved farther inland along the road that led to the Southern Raider Camp, he saw many groups of survivors comforting one another. These were the last of them from the northern camp. Many people gathered around him, and one young girl who had lost her parents ran to him and cried in his arms. He embraced her tightly and softly kissed the top of her head. The Good King stood back and watched. Arlan continued to walk with his arm around her as soldiers saluted him. He began counting his injured clansmen quietly until he was greeted by Mosimer and his men. They had rescued as many soldiers as they could find from the eastern perimeter and were attempting to reunite as many families as they could.

"Prince Arlan!" Mosimer exclaimed, hugging him tightly. "There are only two of you missing now. Your mother has been taken to the southern camp. She has been trying to keep herself busy with all of the injured. She is very worried. Go to her soon and ease her mind."

"I will," he replied, looking around. "Isn't there any news about Nabe and Illiam?" Mosimer sighed. "Hurry and tell me Mosimer! We do not have time to waste!" Arlan exclaimed. "Where were they last seen?" he asked earnestly.

Josem ran to Arlan saluted and then hugged him. "Brother, you're alive! Are you hurt? They said that you were at the Northern perimeter with Urius."

"Yes, I was. We were separated by the rock and flames. Of course, we had to take turns saving one another's lives… and why are you here?" he replied, as he observed Mosimer's and Josem's expressions.

"What else are you not telling me Mosimer? What happened to my brothers? They must be still in the camp."

"Although Nabe and Illiam have not been found as of yet, there is still hope. But Arlan…" Mosimer said in a solemn voice. Arlan moved as though to return to camp, but Mosimer pulled him back. "That's not the worst of it. General Urius is dead," Mosimer continued. "Josepher saw him take his last breath at the bridge."

Arlan's face paled in disbelief. "I…I have to find my brothers," he said, numbed by the shock.

"Then I'll come with you, " Josem replied. In a flash, Arlan grabbed him by the collar and pushed him to the ground. He pointed directly between Josem's eyes and shouted, "You will stay HERE or so help me!" He grabbed a crossbow that leaned against a tree and commanded that someone give him a quiver of arrows that had been laced with poison. He grabbed the reigns of the nearest warring beast and turned to ride back toward the bridge. The only father figure he had left attempted to pursue him by blocking his path.

"Arlan! I can't let you go. Especially not alone!" Mosimer cried. He summoned his beast and mounted it.

"Let him go!" ordered the Good King, who had watched everything.

"I cannot bear to lose any of them," Mosimer pleaded. "I think a part of me dies every time I think of it." Weeping but obedient, he reluctantly dismounted his beast. "I must trust

crouch as the heavy thud on the earth came pounding toward him.

A Drud soldier leaped at him, swinging a sword in his clawed hand and screaming, "Mother is gone! We were many but are no more! Free my brothers!"

The Drud continued to swing frantically, but Illiam evaded each blow. With both of his hands, he grabbed the large, muscular arm that held the sword and brought it as far down to the ground as he could. As the brute fought to free himself from the tight grasp, Illiam lifted himself onto the brute's arm and climbed onto his shoulder so quickly that the brute didn't have time to comprehend what was happening. Illiam wrapped his legs around the Drud's neck. He clenched his hands together, lifted them into the air, and brought them down hard on the back of the Drud's head, so hard that his eyes rolled back. As he began to fall, Illiam remembered that Druds multiply themselves and cannot be killed by beheading. Illiam dealt the final blow by snapping the brute's neck before he could hit the ground. He stepped down off the dead brute and looked at his hands in amazement.

Great One, what is happening to me? he thought. Suddenly remembering Nabe, he pressed his hand to the snow-covered ground. He closed his eyes, waiting to feel what was going on around him through the thick and heavy snow whose icy touch didn't affect him at all.

He found Nabe lying on the ground and easily hoisted him to his shoulder. He didn't realize how large he had become to the point where Nabe looked like a child draped over him. More Druds charged him as he moved toward the bridge, but he easily crushed them with blows that broke and crushed their bones. Illiam looked around again, astonished that he was able to destroy them so easily and without hesitation.

As he trudged through the deep snow that was now up to his ankles, Illiam could hear warring beasts in the distance. As he drew closer to the bridge, he told Nabe, who was still draped over his shoulder, 'We're almost there, brother." In front of him were boulders that stood as high and as intimidating as the brutes who had hurled them into the camp. Illiam observed the obstacles in front of him and laughed. "Great One, these are not made of flesh and blood. How do I move these?" he asked. He waited as the large soft flakes covered him and the Northern Outer Lands in the purest white snow, erasing the stench, ash, and death from the air.

Illiam looked up at the boulders as he felt his brothers' pulse and steady breathing against his warm shoulder. He saw a carving of a handprint appear on one of the boulders. A strong wind blew up behind him, pushing him toward it. He extended his arm and pressed his hand against the carving. It disappeared up to his wrist. Afraid, he pulled his hand back suddenly. He took a few steps back, observing that his hand had taken on the appearance of the rock that the boulder was made of. He shook his hand and found it restored.

The wind behind him blew stronger, pushing him toward the boulder again. He braced himself against it, and it stopped instantly. He stumbled back, almost dropping Nabe in an effort to keep his balance. He successfully regained his stability but was bewildered. "Great One, is this you?" he asked, perplexed. Again, the wind blew behind him, nudging him toward the carving that seemed to extend out of the rock.

Illiam moved forward and reluctantly placed his hand on the carving again. It receded slowly into the boulder, leading Illiam and Nabe safely through to the other side. In disbelief, Illiam looked back for the carving, but it had vanished. He touched the spot where they had emerged from the boulder but saw no trace of an opening anywhere. He stood in awe.

The wind pushed him forward again, and he heard the howling of the warring beasts positioned at the base of the bridge. Tears fell from his eyes.

As Illiam approached the bridge, his jaw dropped. He had never seen anything more majestic in his life. Looking up, he observed all the fine weaving of the thick snow-covered vines and sculptured earth. Its sides were tall. He placed his feet on it, and when he did, his skin changed to the same earth that formed the bridge. He felt the length and width of it with each step. He felt the hollow underneath and felt its height as it stretched high into the sky over him. Once Illiam stepped off the bridge, his skin was restored completely. "You have to wake soon Nabe," he whispered. "You'll never believe what just happened to us." Illiam's heart was so full with wonder he thought it would burst.

After Illiam stepped onto the snow on the other side of the bridge and looked down at his hand. He flexed it once, and it again transformed into the earth that comprised the bridge. He flexed it once more and found it restored to normal. As he moved ahead, he was startled to see Arlan sitting motionless on top of his beast, staring at him with wide eyes. Although he was caught off guard, Illiam waved and tried to put his younger brother at ease. Arlan did not respond. Illiam trudged slowly through the deep snow toward his brother as Arlan's beast howled and resisted slightly.

"A few things have happened since we've been separated brother." Illiam said when he finally arrived at Arlan's side. "There has been some kind of impartation…" he struggled, unsure how to explain.

"I am overwhelmed," was all that Arlan could say. Illiam placed Nabe's limp body gently on Arlan's warring beast. He took a deep breath and returned to the size of a normal man. He flexed his hands and his skin transformed into rock. He squeezed his eyes shut and grew to the height of Arlan astride his beast. Arlan smiled as he watched on in disbelief. Illiam shrugged for the lack of words to explain how he had been able to do such incredible things. He gestured for Arlan to go before him, and they walked together to reunite with their clansmen along the road to the Southern Raider Camp.

Someone gasped as each clansman saw Arlan being escorted by a large mountain of a man. A hush fell over the crowd as others turned to observe what was happening. Everyone there witnessed Illiam's form and was stunned.

"Is that…Prince Arlan?" one asked another.

"What is that with him?" someone asked in horror.

Arlan dismounted and called for his soldiers to attend to Nabe. Josem nudged Mosimer so he would look up and witness what was happening. He ran forward to assist the men who were carrying Nabe. As the Good King approached the two men, Illiam's form was restored before their eyes. The Good King smiled at Illiam and nodded without a word. He embraced the Good King as Arlan ran to Mosimer, who smiled and looked to the heavens shaking his head in wonder.

*****

The last of them set out to travel to the Raider camp in the south before sunset. Many anxiously awaited the opportunity to hear the answers to the many questions that Arlan had assured them he would field when they arrived. Mosimer and Arlan led the way and Josem traveled with the unconscious Nabe. Illiam walked behind them with the Good King so that he could get a few answers of his own.

"Good King, what has happened to me?" he asked. "I've been trying to make sense of it all, but it's very un…" He struggled to choose a word that would best describe what he had experienced. "Unusual?" the Good King suggested.

"Yes, very," Illiam nodded. "At first, I thought that the Druds had affected me somehow and that I had become a brute like them. I felt their footsteps on the ground even through the fire, smoke, and heavy snowfall. I felt everything around me that was connected to the earth under my feet and then through my entire body. I've even walked through rock. What am I?"

"You, like me, are an Earth Warrior," the Good King replied. "You have been entrusted with the authority to command the earth and defend all who dwell on it. From here on, you will see more, hear more, do more, and know more than you ever could on your own.

"You have been changed. My advice is that you practice your gifts and use them only for good. Stay close to the Great One, and he will guide you," the Good King added as he reached down and pulled a random root from the ground. It thickened and extended in his hand and then stiffened into a walking stick. Illiam stopped and searched the ground for something that he could command as well. He looked around and wondered where the Good King had found the root, but he quickly abandoned the effort when he saw that his clansmen had pulled far ahead of him.

*****

As they drew near the camp the next day, they were greeted first by the Raiders who had survived the attack in the north. Mosimer and Arlan were greeted warmly with cheers as the people saw their leaders unharmed. Isha Hilda was escorted to them as soon as the women told her that her husband and sons had arrived safely. Josem ensured that Nabe was taken to a warm place in the Southern Raider Camp and tended to carefully.

When the Good King entered the camp with Illiam trailing closely behind him, the crowd grew silent. Mosimer looked around and asked them, "Where is Josepher?" A soldier ran to Josepher's tent, and after a few short minutes he appeared.

"With the deepest sympathy, we grieve with you Josepher. General Urius was both a brave soldier and a friend," Mosimer said with his hand on his shoulder. Josepher nodded and took in a deep breath.

"Are all our princes well?" he asked Arlan, who answered with a smile.

200

"All are well, and one especially is beyond comprehension commander," he replied.

"Good," Josepher said. "As for Urius, his wife, children, and I...we will bury him along with all the others tonight. He would hate that we've prolonged it."

"Aye, you're right," Mosimer said as the large crowd of the Raider Clan stood together on the same land for the first time in many years. Arlan looked around and cried out to everyone who could hear, "Let us not call ourselves Raiders anymore! We do not raid or plunder! Let us heal, cultivate the earth, and protect it instead. From now on, let this be our seal and our crest. Let it be recorded with heavy but grateful hearts this day, by the mercy of our God, that we are and will always be known as the Residuum."

"Don't forget, we have ten princes and no king to unite us!" Josepher added in response, causing a portion of the crowd to murmur.

"What if you did, Josepher?" Illiam asked. Josepher looked over at him incredulously, his broad arms folded. "What if you had a king from one of the heirs of the former king who would be willing to take his place among you? Would you follow him and the God he serves?"

Josepher raised his brow. "You're not trying to convince me to follow this 'Great One' of yours, are you, my young prince?" he asked facetiously.

"You're already persuaded, Josepher. Admit it! You cannot deny all that you have seen until now," Mosimer replied.

"I'll admit nothing until I see a king! Only then will I concede," Josepher replied.

"Do you, young prince, accept the place that all of your brothers refuse?" Mosimer asked Illiam. "Do you, firstborn of the King of the Hills People, dedicate your life to a people who refused to protect you as a child and abandoned you? Surely, all of your days with the Good King were better than any one day here... Have you now decided to live among us?"

"Mosimer, there was a purpose in everything. Look around you," Illiam said, gesturing toward the people. "None of us have gone unchanged. My place is here." He looked at the Good King, who nodded in agreement.

"Then on this day, all that Urius said is true! I will live to see our people united under one king and one God," Josepher said. Amazed, he knelt on one knee before Illiam with tears in his eyes, and the entire clan of both camps knelt in succession after him.

"Then it is settled," Mosimer declared. "Listen, everyone who is under the sound of my voice, and let it be spread among the Hills, the Plains, the Bog, the Marshes, Boroughs, Outer Lands, Valleys, Rivers, Seas, and Catacombs of Fire that there is a king in the Hills who belongs to the Great One. Who protects and guides with love for the people in humility and in truth." He then turned to Illiam and blessed him. "May each day of your reign help restore a broken past, and love, faith, and forgiveness fortify our people in unity from this day forward."

The people cheered with elation. Many embraced one another as musicians began to play their instruments and people began to dance. It was as though they had forgotten all they had lost and were healed in that very moment.

*****

Illiam saw the Good King standing quietly to the side. A few greeted him, but many were still very afraid. Illiam approached him and observed the crowd. "It looks as if I won't be returning to the Plains as I had intended," he said, humbled. "I have somehow become a king to a people that I love deeply."

"You'll be a good one," the Good King replied. Arms folded, as he sat comfortably on a bench near Josepher's tent away from the crowd. "The people need evidence that the Great One is near. Continue to be an example for them to see and to become as well."

"Will you stay with us a little longer?" Illiam requested. The Good King smiled and nodded.

When evening came, the people solemnly paid their last respects to their fallen clansmen and loved ones. They burned the remaining effects that carried no purpose, buried the bodies and lit torches in remembrance of them. The torches burned until the next morning, despite the brisk wind that left a chill in the air that had seemed to follow them from the north.

*****

Josepher was the first in his family to wake that morning. His mood was most cheerful as he exited his tent and called for his dearest niece and nephew. "Twins! Where are you this morn?" Minutes later, Edenmer and his sister, Alyssa, emerged from the tent adjacent to his and joined him, half asleep, with disagreeable scowls.

"Uncle, why do you insist on calling us twins?" Edenmer groaned.

"Why do you insist on *looking* like twins?" he asked mockingly, causing Alyssa to stamp her foot with hands propped firmly on her hips and Edenmer to clench his fists into a tight knot under his arms that were folded across his chest. "Ahhh, you are finally awake!" Josepher exclaimed. He laughed jovially and snatched the two of them into his arms with a big bear hug as they laughed and struggled to pull free from him. When he finally released them, they ran off screaming and giggling, causing a few early onlookers to laugh as well.

"Urius, look what you have left me with!" he yelled into the sky. "I have screaming twins with your spirit, a nation filled with your tenacity, and..." he paused. "A God with your love. Your Great One you've left with me." He looked around at

205

the new environment before him with a heavy yet joyful heart. "We are all of the same mind."

Illiam stayed with Nabe in the infirmary that morning. He assumed that Nabe had been given a dose of their famed Meraflax along with other salves because of the fragrances that lingered in the room. Arlan found Illiam and saw him adjusting the hide that had been draped over Nabe to protect him from the chill that lingered on the morning air. "Now it is my turn to be by your side," Illiam said as Nabe rested. He looked over at Arlan and asked, "Are all of you like this?"

"Like what, my brother and king?" Arlan asked. Illiam looked at him sheepishly.

"I hope to prove to be excellent at both, brother, but I was referring to the dedication and skill of Nabe, the passion of Josem, and the love for the people as yourself. Are all of our brothers like you?"

"You will see soon enough. Mosimer has sent relief for them from their stations and duties. They're on their way to you now." Illiam's heart leapt. He thought about how rapidly his life was changing. He thought about how the Raiders' lives were now under his care and leadership.

"All of those years I sat by the Good King while he met with the elders of the Plains People within the village. I watched and listened closely to how he handled each matter that came before him, and how wise and delicately he managed every one of them. It was a little intimidating," Illiam admitted. "I'll be looking to you and Mosimer for your experience with our people. Prepare yourself," he said with a smile. Shortly after, Josepher and Mosimer entered the tent.

"There you are, although I should have known," said Mosimer. "Josepher and I have come to inquire of you as king. We're curious to know what your first command will be."

Illiam looked at them, after a short pause and said, "We journey back to the north…and we rebuild."

The End

AUTHOR BIO

Michele Callender is an avid fantasy author with a love of crafting unique and enjoyable stories that reach across multiple generations. A dedicated fan of authors including C.S. Lewis, J.R.R. Tolkien, Francine Rivers and Jane Austen, Michele imbues her stories with the magical charm and sense of wonder that have captivated readers for ages. Michele loves books adapted to the big screen, including fantasy, sci-fi, adventure and a good romantic comedy with Christian values. She has also worked as an educator, specializing in special needs children, and she currently resides in New York.

www.ingramcontent.com/pod-product-compliance
Lightning Source LLC
Chambersburg PA
CBHW060326260626
47160CB00007B/2687